I0676936

Eye of The Diamond-T

✳ ✳ ✳

Bill LaBrie
© 2014

Copyright © 2014 Bill LaBrie
All rights reserved.

ISBN: 0615948782
ISBN 13: 9780615948782

*To Waldo, the mystic one who inspires
from his hidden lair*

1

The Bridge

The two silver rails vanished in the dark infinity below him, and Nick watched the snow fall.

He couldn't see much through the truck's windshield. The steering wheel jabbed into his gut at a painful angle. Almost the entire weight of his body rested on the lower rim of the wheel, and blood had started to rush to his head. He felt the truck sway, creaking as it flexed.

Items from the sleeper cab behind him finally fell, hitting his back and shoulders: His Dopp kit, overnight bag, Thermos—and with a thud and a soft, discordant twang—his Gibson archtop guitar. The frame creaked again. He caught his breath. The truck shuddered, then stabilized. His things—his few personal effects—were pressing him even harder against the truck's controls. His face was only inches from the pitted glass of the windshield, still smeared with rabbit guts. Blood dripped from his right knuckles onto the inside of the glass. His hand throbbed. He strained to take control of his breathing again.

From that angle, he couldn't see much. But little details came through to him in new ways—things he might have otherwise ignored. Like the way the snowflakes had accumulated on the brown earth and started to cover the sleepers. The crystals made the rails even shinier and more resplendent in the headlights. He had never looked at rails that way before. It was from a vantage point looking almost straight down from no more than twenty feet above, with the yellow beams of the truck's headlights giving each an angelic halo. He looked at the rails through the truck's hood ornament: a flying, stylized red letter *T*. It was the emblem of the Diamond-T truck company. The same image was emblazoned on the center of the steering wheel then pressing into his chest.

The truck's engine still hummed—six enormous pistons of the Hall-Scott chuffing at something close to idle. He hadn't thought to hit the kill switch. He looked toward the floor. He could just barely see the key in the ignition, its fob dangling from the switch on the dash. Now, fearsomely aware that the truck was hanging from no more than a splinter of the guardrail on the bridge's span above, he didn't dare move.

He felt the truck sway. It creaked. He breathed slowly, deliberately. The air was heavy with gasoline fumes, and his breath condensed on the windshield. He heard and felt the rear wheels still spinning, still powered, though touching nothing but air.

And he watched the snow falling on the rails below.

He sensed he was being watched, himself: In the corner of his eye -- a human face. Slowly, he turned his head only to see his own driver's license attached to his logbook. It had fallen open from where he kept it between the seats in the cab. His own image had been staring at him, maybe out of pity, maybe out of concern, maybe in some effort to make sense of what had brought him here, hanging from a bridge on Route 66, just outside of Seligman, Arizona.

Only a minute or so earlier, he had been fleeing two men in a black Mercury.

There is a message. You have the key. It still rang in his ears. That's what he said. It had sounded so familiar, and yet it had enraged him in ways he still didn't understand.

He thought back on the men. That strange couple: The older one in a long, gray wool coat and a homburg, the younger in dungarees and a greaser cut. All *message* and *key*. Whatever that meant. Were they back there still? Had they found the ice and spun out into a fiery mess? He couldn't be bothered to think much about it right then. He felt a sharpening tightness in the back of his neck.

What would happen to the load he was hauling? It was so secret that his bosses had refused to even allow him to watch it getting loaded into the box trailer, the one now teetering at the edge of the roadway above him. Was it really what it had appeared to be when he had finally worked up the nerve to open the trailer just an hour or so ago? Numbers and letters. Just numbers and letters. He damned his own curiosity. Some things were better left unknown. Better to just do your job and not ask questions. It had worked that way for five years. The load was listed on the manifest as "paper goods." He should have left it at that. That was enough.

For almost five years, he had hauled "paper goods" from the Argonne Nuclear Lab just outside Chicago to Pomona, California, just to deliver them at night to an unmarked warehouse surrounded by government motor-pool cars, armed guards, and barbed wire. Did the nuclear lab make paper goods? Was paper, too, something that was being improved by atomic science? Who cared? More stuff for the newsreels.

For the last few years -- since he had gotten better -- Nick had honed his ability to let things slide. He had convinced himself "toilet paper" was all he needed to know. And, for five years, he had taken the money for hauling toilet paper. But new questions had come to mind on this trip. This very strange trip.

The men in the Mercury weren't after toilet paper. Or napkins, even.

He felt the engine's heat rising up through the firewall. The gasoline fumes hung in the air. Something in the cab had been soaked in gas. He wondered if he should turn off the ignition. No. Maybe in some remote way, the gyroscopic effect of the engine's spinning flywheel was all that was keeping him in place.

The snow kept falling lightly, peacefully. Each breath fogged the windshield.

Then, the carburetor flooded out and with a *chuff-chuff* and a rattle, the engine went dead. The headlights dimmed, and all was silent but for the crackling of the twin exhausts just outside the cab as the snowflakes hit them and the metal cooled.

Nick held his breath. The pain grew in his chest. He feared the dead spot was going to take him. He had to do something--anything. He turned back to look at himself on the driver's license: Nicholas C. Pente, 508 West Diversey, Chicago, Illinois. 5'10", 180 pounds, eyes blue, hair brown, no corrective vision, normal albumin. Expires on his next birthday. He'd need to make plans to be in Chicago around that time a month from now. If he was still driving and everything...

There he was—the little face with a distant expression in the little picture on the Illinois driver's license. He recognized himself. He was aware. He said those words, under his breath, wheezing from the pressure of the wheel on his chest. They were the magic words of power:

Aware. I am aware. I am aware.

The doctor had taught him about the dead spot. Those twice-weekly sessions, like the dead spot itself, had become just more awkward memories receding into gray infinity. All that remained were the monthly trips to the university health center to have his enzymes checked. That routine was all that reminded him that at one time he had been on the verge of being chucked into the nuthouse. He had followed it religiously...up until this last week, when the combination of a bad snowstorm and a hangover had kept him at home for the day. He had been scheduled for a run to L.A. the next morning. It was OK to miss one, he thought. It was just an enzyme check. He felt fine.

But now he wondered. As he stared at the tracks and they took on an eerie focus—he thought maybe the dead spot wasn't gone after all.

The doctors had called it a mild form of epilepsy. He had lived with it from early adolescence. Nick would now and again hit a lull with no pain or agitation, no grand mal retching and trashing. He'd just stop, and his cerebral engine would fall to a lumpy idle. Sometimes, his hands felt strange to him, like they were someone else's. The world around him looked sharper, smaller, and more focused than usual, as though he were looking into the window of a dollhouse. Whenever it hit, he didn't really know himself as an individual. Something took over, and suddenly, he'd be in the middle of the scene like a puppet: Just another thing among things.

Then, as quickly as it had appeared, it would be gone and he'd pick up where he left off.

And yet, that one doctor in New York seriously recommended—almost *demanded*—that he have part of his brain scrambled with a couple of ice picks. He was just one quack out of many. All but one of them recommended drugs or a lobotomy— all but one.

Almost by mistake, he got a referral to a psychiatrist at the University of Chicago. He remembered walking through that doorway, with the doctor's name in black letters on frosted glass: Dr. M. Kultra. He was the doctor of awareness, a Bohemian who had come to America just after the war and spoke soothingly with the accent of Central Europe. "Aware," he said, again and again. In his darkened office, the doctor slowly trained Nick to counter those dead spots using his own self-awareness. Nick had to remind himself who he was, where he was, what he was doing, that he existed as a human at all. It had become a habit for him.

Nick looked into his own eyes in the photo.

He was aware.

The truck creaked and shuddered and tilted downward even more. His angle of vision on the tracks changed. There was a dampened bounce and more creaking. The men. The trailer. How long had it been, anyway? It seemed like years. Looking back wasn't an option. He didn't know that he would look back, even if he could.

Nick was aware. And as long as he was aware, the fear was kept at bay.

Then, he heard the train.

First came the rumble, and then a blaring horn, and then came the fear. He was aware of the fear.

He strained his neck to look up the tracks. The pain was searing. He could see the length of half a city block, perhaps. The winter sun had yet to rise above the line of the surrounding mountains, and the grayness of early dawn was just starting to show them as silhouettes. In seconds, the snow crystals illuminated with a shaft of yellowed light moving in a swirling pattern, glistening in the train's headlight. The sound of the rumble and horn grew louder, more defined. The rails—those shiny rays leading off into dark gray infinity—now disappeared at the top of the windshield. It was as far as Nick could crane his neck to see as the steering wheel tried to separate his ribcage. But then the rails themselves started flashing, reflecting the swirling light, alternating faster and faster across both silver beams, now at a shorter wavelength as the train approached.

The bridge rumbled. The truck shook. There was sound of bending and tearing metal and popping rivets. He heard the blast of the train's horn and the squeal of the brakes.

Through the reticule of the *T* on the hood ornament, Nick focused on the familiar Santa Fe

Warbonnet paint scheme on the front of the locomotive as it burst into the scene. He saw the glaring headlight, growing larger very fast as the truck plunged earthward to meet the train and the ground. It was the Santa Fe Super Chief—something like an old acquaintance. He thought he might have seen the panicked faces of the engineers. In a split second, the train, the track, the earth, and the shiny surfaces of the rails became suddenly smaller and more focused in Nick's eyes -- as though they were toys, just a model train set.

The steering wheel jabbed him even harder. A burst of flame engulfed his legs, then the rest of him.

He was silent.

All faded to white.

Nothing but white.

2

The Travois

It had been snowing that day in Belgium as well, almost thirteen years before. That snow was far thicker and fell with a ferocity. There was nothing peaceful in it.

In the long march from Normandy, starting almost six months earlier, Nick suffered through wind, rain, and mud as the Allied army made its advance. He was still amazed he had even survived the landing on Utah beach, stumbling over fallen comrades as he ran through a fusillade of German lead. One town after another had fallen to the First Army on the way to Paris, and Nick just kept walking. He had shot his M1 Garand a few times, but never really in anger. As a buck private and the least-experienced member of his squad, he had taken to shadowing the red-haired, doughy-faced mountain of a man who had, in his profane and irascible way, shepherded him.

Nick remembered his first encounter with him when he reported to the base in England a few weeks before D-Day:

"What are you, Pente? Some sort of ginny? Is that a ginny name? Or you a spic?"

"Greek. It's a Greek name, sir"

"Oh, a *fag* then. I see," he said, in a calm tone of mockery that was uniquely his own. "I'm going to call you 'ginny fag,' if that suits yah. You ginny fags put your army in skirts. Seen it myself once." Chuckles came from the other soldiers sitting on benches in front of the Quonset hut. The sergeant gleamed.

"Sir, that's fine, sir." Nick had heard worse.

"Don't call me 'sir,' you silly-ass nigger dog masturbator." He almost cracked himself up on that one. Nick thought he caught the familiar scent of cheap booze. The sergeant's nose was a shade redder than the rest of his face. "Call me 'Balsz.' The name's Balsz." A buck-toothed, slack-jawed skinny boy who had been shining his boots, looked up, whooped and did his version of a rebel yell.

"Balsz, yes, sir."

"And if you fuck up, you're going to get Balsz in your face, you hear me lil' fuck-fuck?"

"Balsz, yes, sir"

"Yeah, don't you forget it."

At this, the other GIs surrounding them erupted in laughter and cat calls. One guy with an ironic grin and horn-rimmed glasses just kept softly repeating, "silly-ass nigger dog masturbator" with a wryly disbelieving expression. Nick was flustered. Balsz put his arm around his neck and jokingly pressed his calloused and bandaged fist against his cheek, and the aroma of cheap whiskey, cigarettes, and body odor was almost overwhelming. When he smiled—and it was usually in response to something obscene he had just uttered—it was as if he could power the whole world with his massively plump cheek tissue. When he was angry, it was like a tornado had knocked over a hydro dam during an earthquake.

At least he hadn't called him "Penis." It had been the favored epithet among the boys in high school and had caused him to hesitate giving his last name to new people he met from time to time. Either "Penis" or "Penny" or "Panty" or "Pansy." He hated them all.

In the months that followed, Balsz saved Nick many times from landmines, booby traps, snipers, and even an out-of-control deuce-and-a-half as they walked along on a road in Alsace. But, whenever it happened, Nick knew he could look forward to a flood of invective that would go on for minutes or, in one case, hours. It was a performance he had almost come to treasure: theater of a sort.

But now, they were in the Ardennes, surrounded by trees and mountains. The snow had made communication difficult and had challenged every movement. Everything that was easy when the weather was clear became difficult in the snow.

Things that were at best difficult became almost impossible.

The retreating Wehrmacht had rallied for one last offensive in this difficult area. The U.S. forces had been caught by surprise.

And now, Nick and his small band found themselves in a narrow valley, cut off from the larger platoon. They had fallen through so many snow-packed false surfaces near the trees that might have afforded them some cover that Sergeant Balsz had decided to take his unit through the center of the valley. "Fuck this shit. Just keep your asses covered," he said as he took a long swig from his canteen.

Nick marched on. He studied the trees and rocks for any sign of movement. Balsz said he hoped to meet up with another unit -- any unit -- on the other side of the mountain. The charts made it look very close—though they had to keep brushing away wet snow to see it. As they walked deeper into the valley, Ronson, the tall, skinny guy from Baltimore who carried the BAR, started singing softly to himself under his breath. He couldn't carry a tune. It sounded like something from Sinatra, maybe. Vago, the short and chubby ethnic kid, who didn't like to talk much about himself, followed on sweep as they walked single file. They could all hear him breathing--wheezing. He usually took sweep. And there was Nick—next to last.

Nick thought he saw something move—something in the distance to their left, halfway up the side of a short incline. Then, the earth exploded around him.

Ronson, Vago, and Balsz all fell to the ground. Nick stayed on his feet. His hands felt funny. The world had become like the inside of a snow globe, and he was a little poorly-painted man standing outside of Santa's Village. Everything around him shone in strangely vivid detail. He felt something like a pinprick in his left arm, looked down, and saw blood staining the ground beneath him.

"Pente! Fuck! Hit the ground! Hit the ground, you . . . *fucking moron!*" Nick didn't move. The blood dripped and made interesting patterns on the snow-covered ground in little dots that got more and more dense beneath him. "Pente!" Balsz was screaming. Nick heard the BAR go off. He sensed that things were happening around him, but could take no action. He noticed his rifle had dropped to the ground near the blood stains. He heard Balsz shout something to Ronson and Vago about moving to cover. Nick felt two enormous calloused and bandaged hands grab him roughly by the head. He fell backward. He was being dragged, jerked backwards through the snow. It hurt—a little. The hands moved to hook under his arms. He heard deep breathing -- wheezing. He saw a thin trail of blood emanating from the spot where he had stood as it gradually retreated in the distance. It was interesting—beautiful in its own way. There was no fear. No agitation.

He thought it looked pretty.

"You *stupid fuck!*" Nick heard Balsz louder than thunder, straight into his ear. "You're going to get us killed! Wake up, asshole! *Wake up!*" And still, the valley retreated beneath him.

Bullets from the BAR flew overhead. In a few seconds, he felt something hard jab him in the kidneys. Nick fell backward, tumbling to the ground behind a rock outcropping. He looked around him. Ronson and Vago were there. Ronson was wheezing as he set the BAR on top of the rock, trying to look everywhere at once. Vago's eyes were as big as they could get, forcing his straight and bushy monolithic eyebrow into something resembling a horizontal parenthesis. He faced the opposite way from Ronson, scanning the hillside behind them and wheezing. Nick lay on his back in the snow behind the rock, and more wet snow fell on his face.

The BAR went off again, peppering something, somewhere, with a storm of lead. "I can't see! Where are they?" screamed Ronson as he let off more rounds. Another mortar round exploded a ways off. It was far enough to do no damage, close enough to let them all know that it was being used sight-in to their position. The next would be closer.

Balsz leaned against the rock, winded. "You fuckers...keep firing...they know where we are... motherfuck...keep firing...Pente, you asshole... what's fucking wrong...*with you?*" Nick looked into the sergeant's eyes. He could see every bloodshot capillary, every little grain within the iris. He could smell bad whisky, bad breath, and B.O. – the scent of fear. Nick's hands were tingling. The snow globe was full of four clumsily painted guys, assaulted by snow and lead. He looked into the face of Sergeant Balsz, his apparent rage taking on an eerie vividness in Nick's eyes.

Balsz straightened to brace himself against the rock. He started to lift Nick up from the ground. "You dropped your fucking rifle. Couldn't you see..."

A rifle shot rang out. A dense, metallic thud followed. Balsz's eyes opened wide for a moment, then darkened. His mouth opened. A torrent of blood spilled out over his jacket. His Tommy gun fell to his side. He collapsed.

The snow globe shattered.

Nick looked at the sergeant's limp form braced against the rock. His eyes were still wide open. Vago reached for him. "The sarge! He's hit! He's hit!" He grasped him by the shoulders and shook him, unfastening his helmet. It had a large dent, a large hole in the center of the dent, and was covered inside by blood and brain matter. Nick looked at his sergeant's face. This was the man who had saved him again and again for six months. Those jowls had finally gone limp.

Nick gathered himself up from the ground, being careful to say behind the rock. Slowly, he reached for the bloody Thompson gun that had fallen from his sergeant's hands. Another mortar round, this one about ten feet away. More bullets whizzed overhead, ricocheting off the surrounding snow-covered rocks. Ronson ducked, and the BAR fell to the ground.

With both hands on the Thompson, Nick rose and turned to the valley. A sparse trail of blood marked the path he had been dragged along only a minute or so before. His eyes turned back to the area he had been scanning when the earth erupted around him. He saw a German helmet, almost indistinguishable from the trees and rocks around it. He straightened himself and got to his feet. No time to plan. He ran down the hill. The German helmet was moving. Nick raised the Tommy gun as he ran, pointed it, and with a *rat-a-tat-tat*, the helmet fell backwards.

Another round grazed his shoulder. It stung. He kept running. He was now in the center of the valley, passing the pool of his own blood, and headed up the other side. Another German helmet and the gray tip of a Mauser appeared. Nick was close enough to see the features of a young blond kid. They exploded in a pinwheel of bloody flesh as the .45 slugs from the Tommy blasted out of the hot barrel. Closer, and another almost-adolescent German with a Mauser fell. Now, Nick crested the top of the rocks that had guarded the German position. The Tommy was hot and spent.

There, beneath him, was the sole remaining German. He knelt near the mortar tube and was about to drop another round. He was older -- balding and maybe about fifty or so, a corporal. His gray uniform was muddy and covered with snow. He looked up. Panic overcame his ice-blue eyes. He held up one hand in a gesture of surrender while pulling the mortar grenade out of the tube and gently setting it on the ground. He said some German syllables Nick couldn't understand. His voice was soft. Nick was still enraged, but collected his senses enough to realize the German was surrendering. He held the Thompson on him and signaled for him to back away from the mortar. As the German smiled and raised both hands, Nick tried to remember the proper procedure for taking prisoners.

But he needn't have bothered.

"Penis, did you get the motherfu..." It was Ronson's high nasal warble right behind him. It startled Nick. He turned away from the German for a fateful moment. When he turned back, the older gray-haired and man had pulled his Luger from his holster and was aiming it. Nick pulled the trigger on the Tommy gun. Still empty. In a singular motion that he could never have repeated in a million tries, Nick leapt over the bodies of the two dead riflemen and landed on top of the German. The Luger discharged in the air. With the butt of the Tommy gun, Nick bashed the man repeatedly on his bare head. He bled and screamed as fell to his knees. Nick followed him to the ground, bashing him again and again. The stock of the rifle broke. The German held up his hands to try to shield himself, but then slumped. Nick continued to slam him with the gun-stock as he fell to the ground and, as if in memoriam, he chanted out words with each blow that channeled his departed comrade, Sergeant Balsz: *"You...fucking...kraut...you...just...fucking...die..."*

The German was dead, his head a collapsed mess of bone fragments barely attached to his neck. Both eyes had popped out.

Nick was panting. The German's blood splattered his face and chest. He turned and back from the German's remains. Ronson and Vago stared at him, holding their weapons limp at their sides, both of them speechless and barely breathing.

Two weeks later, an attaché of General Patton awarded Nick the Purple Heart and the Bronze Star. The wound on his upper arm from the first mortar round was a gash about the size of a half-dollar. The bullet from the rifle had barely broken flesh on his shoulder. When Nick heard he had been awarded the medals, he burst into tears. He tried to refuse them, but the army has ways of making one do things that go against one's better judgment. The medals were buried with his father. Nick didn't talk about them after he was discharged, or about the war in general.

And so this replayed through Nick's imagination as he regained a kind of half-consciousness. As if during a fitful sleep cursed with a half-lucid dream, he came to realize that once again he was being dragged along the ground backward. He was bounced and jostled. It was as though he were on some sort of bed or litter, held at an angle.

There were snowflakes falling on his face and arms. The air was cold. He felt tender at the point where the truck's steering wheel had punched him in the gut. He could see nothing at all. It wasn't blackness; it was nothing. But he could smell the faint scent of juniper. He could feel the cold air in his nostrils. And as he jolted and jerked along the ground, pulled along at a slow, deliberate walking pace, he heard the sound of a stick or sticks being dragged along the rocky earth, and an old Indian voice rhythmically chanting:

Ho te ye-ya ye-ya
Ho te ye-ya ye-ya-eh
Ho si ye-ya ye-si
Ho te ye-ya ye-ya

3

The Space Station on the Texas Plain

In the hours or perhaps days that followed, Nick would occasionally stir in his fever-sleep. When he did, he always felt the same sensation of being dragged, hearing and feeling the sticks as they furrowed the ground under him while the Indian chanted.

The pain in his ribs and belly had gotten even more excruciating. He started to feel what he thought were hunger pangs, but an overwhelming feeling of nausea offset them. At times, his face would feel warmer, as though the sun shone on it. Then, it would get cold again. It felt like a fever, but not quite.

At last, he sensed he had come to a stop. He heard a door creaking open. He felt two sets of hands on him, one set under his shoulders and another behind his knees. He was lifted by these unseen hands and gently set down upon what felt like a lumpy mattress. He writhed in pain and retched. He opened his eyes. There was a trace of light this time, maybe the hint of the outlines of a few shapes—though he thought he might have been imagining it. He felt a blanket cover him, then another. There was the sound of a door closing, and all went dark again. Still exhausted, he shivered back to sleep.

But he was aware.

He was aware enough to know he was dreaming when he looked down at the fuel gauge in his truck and made plans to stop at the new diner and truck stop that had just opened outside of Amarillo.

He knew this had happened in real life, and seemingly, only a day or so before. The dream was a simple replay. He remembered that day, checking his logbook and realizing that he would have an hour or so to burn. It would allow him to top off the two seventy-five-gallon gasoline tanks and get eggs, toast, and coffee. He remembered looking forward to stopping at the remarkable place he had seen rising from the cow pasture in-between grain elevators over the last few months -- the place that contrasted so much with everything else within a few hundred miles. He remembered hearing talk at other truck stops. They said it was finally open.

And there it was: rising up out of the flat prairie before him was the brand new Jet Travel Plaza, jutting skyward like a crashed spaceship partially embedded in the Texas plain. The canopies over the pumps resembled giant triangular steel wings tilted up from the ground. They were still rimmed by sharp traces of pink and blue neon as the early dawn had only started to illuminate the vast sky that surrounded them. In the forecourt near the edge of Route 66, a tall, triangular red column lined with streaks of white neon pointed to the stars. At the top, "Jet" buzzed in red neon against a panel the shape of a distorted kidney bean. The panel, too, was lined in green-blue neon.

Downshifting through the ten speeds of the Roadranger gearbox, Nicke once again heard the turbocharger wind down and the valves in the six massive cylinders of the Hall-Scott reassert their chuffing and gurgling sound as he pulled off the highway.

If there was one part of this job he had grown to love, it was the sound that engine made. Whether accelerating or helping to brake the load on long downhill sections -- like the Cajon Pass as he approached L.A. -- it was the sound of power. It did away with the need for a radio, which couldn't have been heard over the sounds of the turbocharger, the straight-cut gears, and the nearly open exhausts, anyway. It was hypnotic -- that sound.

Usually, he was deadheading back to Chicago, and on the way up the pass, he would work all the gears, often without using the clutch, as the engine ripped up to redline. Sometimes, he could push the speedometer into the unnumbered area, proving that he and the Hall-Scott had somehow gotten this enormous cube to more than one hundred miles per hour uphill. At night, he could see the amber glow on the rocks of the canyon walls as flames belched from the exhaust stacks on the overrun. When Nick would take it in for service, the mechanic at the yard back in Chicago always lifted the hood with the reverence one would expect to be paid to the Ark of the Covenant.

"You see?" Boney Slav Tony would ask Nick in a hushed tone, unlit cigarette dangling from the side of his mouth beneath his thick mustache. "Hall-Scott 400. It 1091 cubic inch. More than thousand. Got a cammer, too. Overhead cam. Racecar don't have that. And look...look...supercharge. No, a regular one. From exhaust. Turbocharge. Like fighter plane. At least five-hundred horse. *At least.* Cummins diesel only one-eighty-five." And he would pause, an expression of awe rising over his lined, grease-stained features as he took a puff from his cig. "So, what you carry?"

"Toilet pap...er...paper products," Nick shrugged, then looked away as he shook his head. "I don't really know."

Boney Slav Tony just looked at him, cigarette limp. It was sacrilege of a sort. It was like using a crucifix as a coatrack.

From that point onward, whenever Nick brought the truck to the yard in Berwyn, Boney Slav Tony would greet him with a salute. "Here, Captain

Pente Paper Products. Five-hundred horsepower. Fast toilet paper delivery for peoples in need!" And he would cackle. Nick didn't care. It was a job. He drove a truck with a giant engine and delivered toilet paper from a nuclear lab. So what?

The truck came to a stop in a parking slot in front of the Jet Travel Plaza. Nick set the airbrake, which made its gratifying *phhht* sound. He grabbed his logbook, swung down out of the cab, locked the door, and walked toward the tall glass doors of this Texas-panhandle space station. From the other side of a barbed-wire fence forming the border with a neighboring farm, a black cow nodded at him and mooed.

The tall, automatic sliding doors opened onto a palace of glass, stainless steel and burnished aluminum. The floor glowed with the aura of neon and recessed lighting. The lights over the kitchen-order window looked like the exhaust ports on F-105s, glowing orange on takeoff. The stools at the counter resembled metal-and-vinyl thrones that would have been at home on the bridge of an intergalactic cruiser.

Busboys and waitresses moved about about in linens white as pure bolts of lightning. The waitresses wore orange aprons and little pillbox hats. The workers seemed slow at this early hour, but still carried themselves with a cheerful efficiency. The floor was polished like a gem. It seemed to have diamonds in it. Music filled the air, faintly echoing off of every hard surface. Each booth and most of the spaces at the counter had their own chrome mini-jukeboxes, where for a nickel, one could hear the latest from Ferlin Husky or Jimmy Rodgers or Roger Williams. Where it sat, the Jet seemed like an outpost of an advanced civilization from another planet.

Nick seated himself at the counter and looked around him. This, this was impressive and new. It was the best America could offer. It was good.

"What can I getcha, hon?" The waitress's nametag said "Greta." She was in her mid-fifties and bore a slight resemblance to Jack Carson, the comedic actor.

As Nick drank down his chicory-infused coffee and polished off a plate of over-medium eggs and bacon with a side of grits, he took note of the people around him. This was unusual for him. He was feeling a certain desire to reflect on his surroundings that morning, only three days out of Chicago. Usually, these meal breaks were fast and oblivious. Nick would validate his logbook and think toward his next stop, longing to be back at work in the safety of the cab. A few stools down was a cowboy in hobnail boots, dust still here and there on his blue plaid shirt. He leaned over his coffee and chain-smoked Lucky Strikes while occasionally groaning, his face locked in a deep frown. At the tables and in the over-upholstered orange vinyl booths, the early breakfast crowd had started filtering in—driver teams in coveralls, old local couples where the men wore crew-cuts and horn-rimmed glasses and their wives had hairstyles that weren't seen outside of Texas after about 1935, a couple of army recruits in their new gray-greens and buzz-cuts, a few Mexican laborers from a Greyhound that had made a stop outside. They had to stand in the corner near the front door. The hostess would seat people who came in after them. They thus were the most space-aged customers in the place, having achieved the power of invisibility. A few salesmen sat at the tables reviewing sample packets and order forms while they wheezed and hacked and ran their hands across their day-old stubble. Nick lit a cigarette. The people didn't match their surroundings. They should have all been wearing tunics made from aluminum foil. And Plexiglass helmets.

In the background, he caught little snippets of conversations about the price of hay and the high-way patrol and Wanda at the bowling alley and little Dale going into Cub Scouts and the Peace of the Lord and God's judgment and broken axles and Sputnik and cancer and the early frost and possibility of snow and Pastor Fraley down at First Baptist and suspected communists in the local Kiwanis club and the John Birch Society. Everyone was chattering about something.

Except for two men.

Looking over the few people seated at the tables in the center of the restaurant, Nick watched an ample-hipped waitress filling two coffee cups at a booth at the large front window. As she stepped away, she revealed two men sitting across from each other. One was in his mid-fifties. He was balding, the back of his head rimmed with a graying halo. His eyes were icy blue. He was tall and sat bolt upright in the booth. His expression was flat, and his face had a thickness to it that recalled something like Eastern Europe. Across from him sat a much younger man. He wore black Levi's and a white t-shirt partially covered with a green plaid jacket shirt. He wore his greasy hair in the manner of youth at the time—combed into what they were calling a "duck's ass." He seemed nervous as he slouched and smoked a cigarette with his right hand. His left arm wrapped defensively around his middle. His left knee bounced as he smoked. He seemed to be trying not to look in Nick's direction. The two men said nothing to each other. The older man was stoic as he fondled his coffee cup, twisting it silently in its saucer. Nick turned back to his coffee as Greta refilled it. He lit another cigarette. He sensed the older man's head turning in his direction. The younger man straightened up, slightly. His leg still bounced.

Someone took a seat next to Nick. It was a girl, maybe in her mid-twenties. She had dry black hair—dull in its blackness—and looked as though she had slept against a car window overnight. She was wearing semi-flamboyant sunglasses and a coat that was supposed to look like navy surplus but was cut too well. Her pale face was smooth as china, and she wore a sheen of foundation she seemed to have just freshened. Her deep red lipstick contrasted with everything around her. It didn't do much to offset the unflattering curl of her upper lip, which almost seemed to touch the bottom of her nose. She looked at Nick with a slight sneer resembling a smile—just enough to acknowledge him—then looked back at the area behind the counter, as though searching for something. Her gaze shifted back to the counter and the little stations that held the menus and sugar and condiments, and she seemed to be seething through her teeth in a mildly irritated way. Nick smiled and nodded at her, then flexed his eyebrow and turned back to his logbook. The girl seemed fidgety as she picked up the menu, perusing its cheery depictions of eggs and grits and corned beef hash and pancakes. She groaned to herself.

A minute later, she was joined by a guy of about her same age. A bit plump and slovenly, he wore an army surplus coat that clashed with his thick, blonde beard. His hair was greasy and unkempt, and he had a trace of acne. His striped shirttails hung beneath his jacket and partially covered the seat of his worn jeans. He also wore sunglasses—dark Ray-Bans. He took a seat next to the girl.

"This place is a gas. You should see the shitter," he said as he spun around on the stool, eventually facing her. She was still looking at the menu.

"What's good to eat here? I don't see *anything* that's not fried," she said in a voice straight from some burg in the middle of Long Island. Her voice was cigarette-gravelly and nasal.

"Yeah, not much," said the guy as he swung side-to-side by his hips on the stool in a distracted, juvenile kind-of way. The front half of his body was on the counter. Greta the waitress came back, looking at him sternly. He managed to seem both ebullient and sullen at the same time.

"What can I get you, sir?" she asked. One could always tell when a Texas waitress didn't like a male customer; she called him "sir." Everyone else was "hon" or "babe" or "darlin'."

The guy slowly straightened himself up and jerkily looked at her and in various other directions. He glanced down at the menu. "Uhh..." he said, deep in concentration as he pulled on his beard.

Johnny Mathis sang "The Twelfth of Never" in the background.

"Do you have hummus?" asked the girl, finally.

"Humma...do you mean hash? We have hash."

"It's like chickpeas. All ground up and with... no?" Greta was holding her order pad and looked at the girl with a frown as she shook her head.

"We have peas. Want a side of peas?"

"Nah," said the girl with a long nasal drone, returning her gaze to the menu.

"Sir?" asked Greta, looking back at the guy, who by now was trying to light a cigarette while thoughtfully twisting his earlobe.

"Just coffee. That's cool. Yeah. Thanks," he grunted, apparently barely awake.

Greta restrained herself from rolling her eyes too much as she poured him a cup.

"Do you have Sanka?" asked the girl.

Greta silently turned around and grasped the pot with the orange handle from the burner.

"Oh, that's OK, I just..." Greta had already poured her a cup with the little orange-rimmed doily in it. She set it down in front of her and walked away.

Agitated, the girl turned to her companion and said something under her breath, still managing to sound nasally. "I was just asking if they had it, I didn't want it right now. I might have wanted it later. What kind of joint is this? Shit." She was fuming.

"You know, sometimes I think the whole country is, like, turning into one giant bowling alley," said the guy through some thickness in throat. And by that, he meant, well, nothing, really.

The girl looked back at her cup of Sanka, disconsolate at getting a cup of decaffeinated coffee she might have wanted later, or might not have wanted after all. She glanced around her, looking like she felt put-upon by her surroundings.

"Yeah, I know. It's like you can have whatever you want, as long as it's plastic and shoved down your throat."

"Bowling alley...bowling..."

"I don't know how Kerouac put up with this shit. I mean, why bother?"

"Discover America. See the USA in your Chevrolet." He made little bopping sounds with his lips.

"My ass." she said in a matter-of-fact way. Nick glanced down beside him to see her thighs, encased

in black polyester Capri pants, flowing over the side
of the vinyl-covered stool. Her ass wasn't much to
look at.

The girl lit a cigarette, silently borrowing
a lighter from her guy. He sipped at his coffee,
stretching and cracking his neck now and then.

After a minute, he seemed to be coming back
into some sort of consciousness. He straightened
up on the space-aged vinyl barstool.

"Hey, Sher," the guy said. "Guess what?"

"What?"

"I heard something big." He was keeping his
voice low -- almost whispering. His demeanor was
still that of a kid whose sugar high had peaked an
hour before.

"About what?"

"Big buy. Big stuff. Hard stuff. Big, big, big."

"Who? Who told you? What?"

"Lacroix. Big L."

"Where, what?"

"Crazy shit. Shit I never even heard of. Just letters and numbers and shit."

"So?"

"So, guess where he got it?"

"Troy, don't do this to me, please. I haven't
had anything decent to eat in days and probably
won't until we get to Chicago or maybe even back
to Brandeis." She sounded irritated and not in the
mood for his childish crap.

Troy lifted his sunglasses to reveal bloodshot
eyes with dilated pupils. He looked at her with a

conspiratorial tilt to his bushy brow. He raised his hands between them, and tried to make out some letters in semaphore code with his fingers. He could tell he was taxing her patience even further, so he resorted to saying the letters under his breath as he tried to make them with his hands.

"*See...aye...aaaayy. See...aye...aaaayy.*"

Sher looked at him, nonplussed.

"The CIA is selling shit?" she asked.

It was way too loud for the high, nasally tone she was using. Troy nervously dropped his sunglasses back down and looked around behind them. He glanced at Nick, who was buried in his logbook—or pretending to be.

"Sher, shut your trap. This place is a rhomboid. It's not even square. Keep it low, babe."

"Why would—"

"L says...this is what he says...he says that the *see...eye...aaayy* is testing out some new shit on people. Shit that they just used on political prisoners and whatever. But now they want to try it on normal people—squares, even, someday—but starting with junkies. They've got, like, factories for it now with, like, Nazis working there. And they're talking about moving so much shit at once that he's like, thinking...what do you want me to do with this shit? You going to pay me to put it in the water supply? They expect him of move this shit on the street. And they say they want money for it, eventually. Capitalist with a capital 'K.' Your government at work."

"Where? New York?" She pronounced it "noo yawk."

"No, L.A. And the problem is...the problem is that no one knows this shit. It doesn't even have a real name yet. So, how do you sell it? It's not like someone is going to walk up to you and ask to score some NKD-whoosie-watzid. NKD-something. I dunno... crazy...loco...so, he's like giving it out free to anyone who'll take it now, even though he couldn't even tell me what it was like, I mean, what it did. He said it was real hard to describe. So, he was trying to use it to cut horse or coke or speed, but he said something about it causing real coo-coo weirdness that way. I mean, shit you don't want to know about."

"Did you score?"

"Nah...not my thing...all I had to hear was *seee aye ayy*, and I was out. Screw them."

Sher was already bored. It was a Troy thing. She looked around at the lamps and decorations and blew smoke out of her nose. She started flipping through the selections on the mini jukebox at the counter. "Well, I'm glad we're out of that scene. L.A. was getting just too weird. Anyway, my mom is expecting us Saturday at her place in Lincolnwood. My dad might be there with his new girlfriend. So, you're going to need to wash up and stay straight for a while. Oh, look at this; they have 'Cherry Pink and Apple Blossom White'." Troy stubbed out his cigarette and lit another. In response to her chiding, he shrugged and nodded in an exaggerated way that called to mind a chimp.

"Troy, I'm serious. Don't give me this."

Nick had heard enough. No wonder he tended to ignore most of what went on around him, especially anything that came out of the mouths of beatnik wanderers. He took another sip of coffee and neatened the tails of some of the sevens on his log sheet.

CIA mind control was a nice angle, though. Paranoia to the right of him, paranoia to the left of him, paranoia all around him. Quietly, he chuckled as he looked at his watch.

The jukebox started playing a big hit from earlier in the year. It was "Round and Round" by Perry Como. For most of the summer of 1957, you couldn't go far without hearing its cheery polka-like rompiness from every jukebox and car radio. It seemed suited to the spirit of this place, this time in history, if not the decor:

Find a wheel, and it goes round, round, round,
As it skims along with a happy sound!
As it goes along the ground, ground, ground,
Till it leads you to the one you love!

But after Perry had crooned through a couple verses, the record stuck. *"Round and roun-round and roun-round and roun..."* Nick looked up at the speakers, which were styled to look like electric razors that had been styled to look like automobile grills that had been styled to look like parts of fantasy rocket ships. He smiled. His gaze returned to the two men at the table. They both turned to look at him, abruptly. The older one curled his lips into something resembling an imitation of a pleasantry. Nick shook his head and chuckled. Still it went on *"Round and roun-round and..."*

The manager—a balding, heavy middle-aged man in a white shirt and tie--yelled from the cashier stand back behind the counter. "Mabel, can you fix that? The dang record's got stuck again! Does that every dang time!" There was laughter from most of the other customers, but not the two men at the booth.

At the counter, Troy was snickering with his lady friend. "Perry Como. Just another *fucking* capitalist tool. Just repeats and repeats and repeats. Same shit. Do what they tell him," he said, softly but with a condescending tone that smacked of the superiority of the one who "got it" when forced to be around those who never, ever would. Sher laughed her nasally laugh. At that, the cowboy in the hobnail boots got up and walked to the couple, passing behind Nick, boots clacking on the hard floor as he sauntered.

"Sir," he asked, politely but firmly, still wearing a deep frown. Troy tried to ignore him. He didn't turn around. "Sir," the cowboy repeated. Troy kept talking under his breath. The cowboy reached down, grabbed the edge of the seatback, and yanked the stool around forcefully. It stopped when Troy faced him. Troy's sunglasses fell off halfway. He jolted and looked up at the cowboy through bloodshot eyes. "I'll ask you *once* to kindly mind your tone in this here establishment," said the cowboy in a deep drawl.

Troy looked at him, put his sunglasses back on, slowly straightened his jacket, then spat on the floor directly in front of him, looking up at cowboy after they both watched his brownish spit sully the jewel-like floor.

There was a moment of peaceful silence between the two. All eyes were on them. Perry still crooned in the background. *Round and Roun... Round and Roun...*

"Why . . . you *boshevikin' sonofabitch*," said the cowboy, rather calmly, all told, as he grabbed Troy by the head and violently threw him to the floor with all of his strength, as though he were about to tie a recalcitrant steer. Sher screamed. The cowboy reached down, grunted, and grabbed Troy by his jacket, dragging him across the diamond-like floor. He flung him towards the front doors, kicking him in the ass as he tumbled. The doors opened just in time to allow Troy to roll through them. He came to rest on his back on a small shrub to the side of the entry. Sher was still screaming as she ran after him. The cowboy walked back, reached into his pocket, pulled out a two-dollar bill, set it on the counter, and tipped his straw hat to Greta. A few couples and salesmen at the tables got to their feet and applauded. There were various *"whoop!"* sounds from here and there.

Round and roun-round and roun-round and roun still spilled from the speakers.

The doors slid open again. It was Troy. His sunglasses were broken and half-hanging on his face. His bottom lip was shuddering. He looked around at the people the tables, and in a vocative tone that tried hard to be thunderous but just sounded wheezy, he addressed them: "You *fucks!* All you squares are getting screwed! You don't know what they're doing to you! You're all going to get it up the ass. Your minds are being controlled by capitalists and your own government. You sit here eating your *pigs in a fucking blanket* and—"

Two beefy guys in dirty dishwasher uniforms and caps ran out from behind the counter and grabbed Troy—one under each arm--dragging him outside. By then, the cowboy had sat back down at the counter. He looked over his shoulder. He groaned again.

"Check, please," said Nick, taking a last sip of coffee as he checked his watch.

As he walked back to the truck, he walked past the two dishwashers holding Troy up against a rusty gray '48 Studebaker coupe with luggage tied to its roof. A third was punching him in his face and gut. He moaned and cried loudly, and was starting to bleed from his nose and mouth as the car shook with every punch. Sher stood a few steps away from him, screaming but still holding a cigarette. She was hysterical and bouncing on her high heels, searching around her for help that wouldn't arrive.

Her ass really isn't much to look at, thought Nick as he walked by.

Nick moved the truck under the large wing-like canopy to one of the gas pumps. An attendant walked out to fill its tanks. As the *ding-ding-ding* of the pump continued unabated, the attendant was moved to conversation.

"Wahl, sir, that's a whole lotta Ethyl. Ahh didn't know them things still ran on gasoline. And you're running that expensive stuff, too!"

"Yeah, glad I'm not the one paying the bills for it." Nick was updating his logbook with gas facts and tire pressures. He didn't bother looking up.

"That's sure right. Hey, let me ask yah this, if yah don't mind: You ever get scared about all this here gas?"

"Scared?" Nick looked at the attendant -- just a kid in overalls.

"Yeah, you know. Hunnert and fifty gallons of gasoline raht underneath yah thar. Car could hit yah or somethin'. You know what I'm talkin' 'bout? Diesel don't blow up or nothin'."

"No, I don't get scared."

Nick glanced up, a tire gauge in his hand. In the distance, he could see the two men from the booth walking out to their car. It was a black Mercury. They seemed to be trying not to look in his direction. They walked in single file, the older one trailing the younger.

Nick left the Jet. About three miles later, he thought he heard a tire coming apart on the back of the tractor. He pulled over in a roadside clearing just past a grain elevator. He looked in his mirrors before opening the door. A black Mercury pulled off the road behind him, far enough back so he could barely see it though the glare of the sun rising over the Texas plain.

4

Why is That Important?

The wind whistled through the walls, and the parts of his face that were exposed told him the room was cold.

These were good things. There were no drafts in coffins. And he had heard that six feet under the earth stayed relatively warm. Warmer than it was in that drafty room, at least.

He opened his eyes. The dim shapes he had seen before he drifted off to sleep had become clearer. And now, they were in color. *Yes!* He saw a blue shape, vertical, and to the side above where he lay. The way it moved made him think it was a curtain covering a poorly sealed window. In the background, he heard or, perhaps, sensed something. Another person. He heard the shuffling of a foot and maybe the creaking of a chair. He cleared his throat. It was so dry that he instantly groaned and coughed in a short fit.

"You 'wake now, eh?" The voice was old and slow and had the unmistakable accent and broken rhythm of a Pueblo Indian, an old Indian man's voice. Maybe Zuni. Maybe Hopi. Maybe Navajo. He had heard it at every truck stop along his route through Arizona and New Mexico.

The chair or whatever it was made a creaking sound again.

"I...can't see anything...where..." Nick's voice was wheezy and clotted.

"You here on farm," came the response, slowly, and in that measured, distinctly accentuated way old Indians spoke English. It had a texture to it. It sounded like the land looked.

"Where? Seligman?"

There was a long pause.

"You mean *Thavgyalyal*?"

"I mean Seligman. Seligman, Arizon—" Nick started coughing again. He heard someone get up and move.

"Frendt, you need water. Take some water." Nick felt both his hands guided to a rough cup. To his shaking fingers, it felt made of clay. The water tasted sweet and pure, more so than any he could remember. He drank the cup down. His abdomen was still burning from the steering wheel, but it had subsided from the retching he felt before and moved on to something resembling deep soreness.

His legs felt strange. They wouldn't move. He felt like he was encased in concrete.

"How did I get here?"

"I bring you. Big accident."

"I know, but how?"

"I saw you there and think you need help. So, I bring you here."

"Why not a hospital? Do the cops know?"

There was silence.

"Why do you care about that?"

Nick was at a loss.

"My truck. I have a load in the truck. It's really important. I gotta get back to Seligman."

"Frendt, I don't think you got a load now," came the reply. "What was load?"

"Paper goods. I think."

There was a long and awkward silence.

"Don't sound too important," said the voice, finally.

Nick was still burning from the steering wheel and still enervated. But he was getting ticked off anyway.

"Look, whoever you are, I—"

"Bacho. They call me Bacho."

"OK, Bacho. Thanks for bringing me here. Thanks. I really appreciate it, but right now, I don't know where I am, and I can't see and my legs. . ."

"You here."

"Where is here?"

"The farm. My land. I live here long time. My people--"

"I can't see any—"

"You can't see with eyes. Other ways to see."

Nick was about to react with anger when he suddenly realized his mind had assembled a composite image of every old Indian man he had ever seen in the movies and on TV and hanging out in front of truck stops begging for change and passed out drunk on the streets of Gallup and working at trading posts and demonstrating weaving for tourists and in his various books for college classes on anthropology he had dropped out of when the dead spot had gotten to be too much, while at the same time discarding the portrayals by actors like Ed Ames and Jay Silverheels and Rock Hudson, who he knew looked nothing like real Indians. Suddenly, Bacho was there, just as he had been since Nick first heard the chanting while being dragged to this place.

Nick remembered things he had read in college, half-completed courses during his fitful, barely remembered attempts at higher education. He remembered things about Indians and how they lived in the pueblos of the old Southwest. At times, he had looked out of the truck at their ramshackle settlements or seen them riding in the beds of pickup trucks as he sped past. And he had wondered how much longer they could possibly live that way out there, like that. They were curiosities to him and the rest of the world—the remnants of a once-great civilization brought low by firewater and technology.

"And you know what I doing now."

Nick listened carefully. There was a scraping sound, and the sound new shoelaces make when you thread them through the eyelets. At regular intervals, there was a soft *thunk* as the reed battened the last thread against the fell.

"You're...weaving a rug?"

"*Hey-yeah*...I weave rug. Did this long time." The voice continued, blandly.

Nick pictured an old Indian man—the ideal old Indian man—crouched in front of a rustic loom, threading colored strands from one side to the other. And with each sound, he saw in his mind another thread making its way through the warp and getting packed down against the previous strand in the woof.

"You know it's cold here. Sorry 'bout tha. It's cold. Snow a little. So, you know, you on the mountain, right?"

"Right." Nick couldn't understand how these explanations had somehow satisfied him, at least in some minimal way. He found it somewhat troubling. He let it slide. He turned his head and saw more shapes, colors, movements. All was blurry. He remembered that distorted kidney-bean shape from the sign at the Jet. Everything in the room looked like distorted neon kidney beans. Some of them were moving, like the curtain above him.

"How far are we from Seligman? Or Thav..."

"Thavgyalyal? Oh, not too far. About day."

"On foot?"

"Yeah."

"Do you have a car? Truck?"

"No, only sheep."

"Do you have a phone?"

"No, no phone."

"How do you...do anything with the rest of the world?"

There was a pause as Nick tried to wrap his head around where he was and why he was here.

"Why is that important?"

"I need to get back"

"Hey, you got family?"

"No. My mom died during the war, when I was in Europe. My dad died after I came back. A little while after." Nick wasn't sure why he was sharing this.

"No wife? No kid?"

"No."

"Girlfriendt?"

"No."

"Boyfriendt?" The question came with a distinct lack of any provocation.

"No!" Nick was getting irked again. "What in hell does this have to—"

"Then why is it important? You lie down and get better. You sleep. I back soon."

Nick saw a light blue kidney bean shape move above him, with a reddish-orange shape on top of it and felt two large, strong, hands on his shoulder gently push him back down to the bed. His gut still burned with pain. Before he fully reclined, he looked out beyond the foot of the bed to where most of the light was coming from. The door was open. Through the doorway, he could see another teal blue kidney bean shape. This one had a shape he found somewhat more familiar and definite, and it moved the way a woman's skirt moved with her hips.

Then, the door closed, and it got dark again. Sleep came once more.

5

Euridice

There was no crisp replay of any past event this time. His dreams consisted of images similar to what surrounded him in the room while awake—floating kidney beans of various colors. Some floated in a stately way, while others darted and bounced. It was like watching an overpopulated aquarium full of the most colorful salt-water-dwelling specimens, some swimming in miniature schools, others making their own way through the multitude. T here was no unifying theme. All were celestial blobs of pastel shades against a white backdrop.

For years, dreams, any dreams at all, had been rare for Nick. In the preceding five years, if he did indeed have dreams, he hadn't remembered them the next morning. He assumed that it was because most of his rest occurred in the sleeper bunk of the semi-tractor. But, really, he had noticed it shortly after he started therapy with Dr. Kultra, before he started driving. Before visiting the doctor, he had been constantly troubled by vivid dreams, some of them lucid. Some concerned the war, but not all. At times, he would stay awake for days, hoping that whatever it was in his waking life that caused the dreams would pass, and he could finally get some rest. But he never knew what would set off these dreams. They usually had nothing to do with whatever stresses he experienced as a sparsely employed veteran with an interesting psychiatric problem.

The therapies Dr. Kultra introduced seemed not only to have stabilized his mentality during his waking hours but to have also ironed out his subconscious.

Nick felt something warm and damp on his face. A cloth wiped his forehead and cheeks, dipped to his ears, and dabbed around his neck. He heard water trickle into a bowl in between strokes as his skin cooled. He stirred. A hand gently rested across his chest. As he returned to consciousness, he remembered the last time he had felt so tenderly attended. That one; she had left him like the others. It was after her that he had stopped trying. He made himself believe driving was enough. He hired help when appropriate. When in Chicago or L.A., he paid girls not so much to come to him, but to leave when he was finished. That made it seem better somehow.

He slowly opened his eyes. What he beheld ripped through his very core: The face of a specter. White as a sheet, with massively enlarged dark caverns that might have been eyes, and a surface that appeared to be made of withered clay. It hovered above him. The mouth opened and seemed to engulf souls while regurgitating their mangled remains. It wore a long ceremonial red robe. Rolls of tumescent flesh gathered under what appeared to resemble a chin. A smile both wicked and wan came over its horrid mouth as it seethed.

Nick shook. He jerked upwards, and a gasp left his lungs. He cried out. He tried to sit up. He turned his head and flexed his neck looking for an escape. His legs wouldn't move. The figure had risen above him. He couldn't move. He lay there petrified. He gathered everything inside of him to turn back and face it.

He forced his eyes open. And before him, what had been the specter-face had somehow transformed into the most exquisitely beautiful girl he had ever seen. He gasped and panted. The girl had stood up, startled by his sudden movement. She still held a damp cloth and a bowl. She looked into his eyes. Her eyes were brown, with a hint of something else, maybe saffron. Her skin was the color of caramel. Her full lips flexed in a shy pout. Her black hair was pulled into whorls on either side of her head, which were wrapped around some circular ornaments. Nick recalled from some book or documentary he'd seen during his brief college career that they were ceremonial to the Hopi people. Unmarried girls wore them. She wore a long red skirt and a rough cotton blouse. It clung to curves that hinted at the pert fulsomeness of youth. Her body was in its girlish prime. She was perhaps nineteen and just old enough to seem fully-grown -- on the verge of womanhood. She stood with an expression of mild dismay and shyness, but no fear at all. She gazed at him with wonder, making him feel like she cared for him and, most of all, that she was aware of him. He hadn't felt that for so long. It was likely he had never really felt it before at all.

Finally, Nick cleared his throat. "What are you doing here?" he asked. She moved back to the side of the bed and dipped the cloth into a clay bowl full of water.

"I live here," she said. She wrung out the cloth.

"Are you—"

"Yes, I'm his daughter," she said, anticipating his question. Her voice was less accented than her father's, but still seemed very native, bearing the same broken cadence. There was a soft, knowing innocence in it.

Nick looked at her. He sensed deep warmth inside of him. Something made him want to reach out to her, to surrender to her in a way that he really couldn't imagine.

"What is your name?"

"My name is Euri."

"I am Nick. . ."

"I know," she said. She could see he was astonished. She smiled, embarrassed. "I read your shirt while you were sleeping," she admitted. She leaned forward to wipe his face again. Nick's blue uniform shirt with the red piping was draped over a chair near the door behind her.

"Where are we?"

"On my father's farm." The cloth gently rubbed against his nose and traced his lips.

"OK, but where is—" he stopped.

She looked at him. He could sense what she was going to say, or at least thought he could. He caught himself hoping his questions wouldn't arouse in her any impatience that might drive her away or even make her stop washing him for an instant. "Well," he said. "I guess I would need to tell you why I think that's important."

Her eyes moved down and up again as she smiled in a timid little way. Then, she washed his neck, taking gentle care of his throat and working her hands along his collarbone, allowing her hand to feel one of his well-muscled shoulders, near where that German bullet had grazed him thirteen years before. He felt the back of his left hand move against her thigh as she moved to sit next to him.

And then, like a flash, the hunger pangs took him. He felt hollow inside—as empty as a cave. He hadn't eaten, possibly for days. His expression must have changed. Euri got to her feet as he nearly writhed, and she turned and walked out of the hut. The door creaked behind her. "No, Euri!" cried Nick. He was almost ashamed to be calling after her. He didn't want her to leave. Leaving was the worst possible thing she could have done at that moment. He would have rather she had slapped him or poured the water on his head, or even punched him in his still-sore gut. He wondered if his hand against her nubile thigh had been too forward. He looked around the hut. It was as rustic as he had imagined: unpainted wood slats for walls, with more of them on the floor, blankets hung on the walls and over some windows, simple handmade furnishings, a potbelly stove, and what he discerned was the old man's loom against the wall opposite Nick's bed, covered in a dusty sheepskin.

Bacho wasn't there. Nick was alone. In a fit of utter helplessness, he called out for Euri. He felt his legs, but when he tried to move them, they just wouldn't do more than twitch.

The door opened. Euri was there. She held a pottery bowl. Nick could smell something delicious. Euri smiled and quickly brought the bowl to him. With a wooden spoon, she stirred as she sat down on the bed beside him. He pulled himself upright on his elbows.

"Lamb," she said. "You eat lamb? This is mutton. Grown-up lamb."

"Yes, yes." And with that, she filled a spoon with this utterly glorious, primitive stew of hominy, potatoes, and lamb and brought it to his mouth.

He paused, looked at her gorgeous brown-red eyes again, and opened his mouth.

In the hour or so that followed, Nick learned that Euri had been born on the farm. Her mother had died some years earlier. Her father had raised her in the time since. Her mother and travelling missionaries had taught her to read. They had been welcomed until an event that she only described as "the bad time." She had never left the farm beyond a few trips into the mountains that surrounded it.

"So, you have never gone to school?"

"No, there is no school here. I have books. They teach me." Nick looked around the hut. No bookshelf. No stack. Not even a novel spread open on the bed near the door where he surmised Euri slept.

Euri was shy and tentative. "I...I will show you my books." She got up from the bed and knelt down, lifting a red and gray rug that resembled a tapestry of beautifully woven stars. It covered about half of the floor of the small hut. Under it was a wooden door. She lifted it. Below were hundreds of books in several rows, filling the space in between the floor joists. Euri avoided Nick's gaze of astonishment.

The missionaries had left her a Bible and some other spiritual readings and schoolbooks, but her father brought her whatever printed material he could find during his visits down the mountain. He had done this for years. Sometimes it was just a newspaper. In other cases, it was a high school chemistry book or a potboiler pulp novel or a discarded girlie magazine. Once, he brought back a stack of multiple copies of travel brochures and maps that Nick recognized from a Texaco station. Then, there was a windfall: a leather knapsack full of a semester's worth of reading at an elite liberal arts college: Sartre, Plato, Locke, Nietzsche, Flaubert, Rousseau. Nick could recall at least starting to read most of those authors at one time or another. Among these volumes was wedged a NAPA auto-parts catalogue from 1952. All the books, magazines and catalogues were fastidiously arranged in alphabetical order.

"How many of these have you read?" he asked.

"All."

"You've read them all? All of these?" She nodded at him and looked away, shyly smiling. Looking down from the bed, Nick recognized the spine of a book he remembered from years earlier. It was Milton's *Paradise Lost*. It was even the same edition. "I've read that one." He smiled. "I read it in college."

"You've been to school?" Euri asked, excitedly.

"Yes, I've been to school. To college." Nick stared at the book. He remembered wandering around after his discharge from the army, after he no longer had a reason to stay in Chicago. He ended up enrolling as a freshman at a small college in Pennsylvania, on the GI Bill. Those were the bad years, when his dead spot was acting up all the time. Thanks to the constant distraction of bouncing from one flare-up of his dead spot to another, he hadn't lasted long. But he knew enough to realize what Milton was about. Milton and quite a few others. He and Euri gazed at the books in silence.

"Do you have a family?" asked Euri.

"No, not anymore."

"No father? No mother?"

"No." He could tell she wasn't satisfied with his response. "Look," he said, preparing to excuse himself from telling the story he had shared with few others, and really no one since Dr. Kultra. "It's pretty sad. I don't usually want to remember it. I don't want you feeling sorry for me."

Euri's eyes darted. Her jaw grew tense. She pursed her lips. He had known her no more than an hour, and already holding anything back from her was an affront to the intimacy they shared. He gazed at her. He surrendered.

"I was an only child," he began. "My mother lost four kids before me. Four babies, before they were born. All I remember about her was that she was drunk most of the time. And when she wasn't that drunk, she was yelling. My dad usually had to put her to bed. Most days she never got out of bed. My dad raised me. I hated living there. I hated the way I grew up. But my dad made sure we both had what we needed. He looked after us. He was an optician. Glasses, you know?"

Euri nodded.

Nick breathed deeply and then went on. "So, when I got to be sixteen, the war had just started, and I wanted to get away so badly that I bundled up my stuff one night and went to leave. I wanted to sneak into the service. My dad caught me and wouldn't let me go. He wouldn't let me leave him with my mother by himself. He broke down and cried. I felt sorry for him. So, I stayed. I went to school until I was eighteen, then after I graduated, I joined up before I even got drafted. My dad still didn't want me to go, but he knew I was going to get called up anyway. So, I went to basic training, then shipped off to Europe, where...well... When I got back, I went home -- home to Chicago. I had things to show my dad and my mom. I had medals and pictures.

"When I got home, my dad was waiting to meet me. He told me my mother was dead, and how now, he had no one else. I didn't know what he was talking about. He said it happened while I was in the army. She had died a few months before, He said he had told me in a letter, but I never got that letter. He had sent other letters since that time and never mentioned my mother being dead, so I knew he was lying. He broke down and told me that he didn't want me to be sad and distracted in the war, and that he was so afraid to lose me. I was sad and angry at the same time. I was sad about my mom, because even though she was drunk all the time, she was still my mother. And I was angry at my dad for not telling me, for lying to me. So, I ran off. When I came back the next day, the car was running in the garage. My dad was in there. He was dead. He killed himself."

Euri put her hand on his shoulder. He gasped. A wave of comfort came over him. He put his arms around her and fell back on his bed. Euri followed him, her arms wrapped around him. He felt tears but couldn't tell if they were tears of sorrow or joy, nor if they were hers or his. Soon, sleep came again.

6

Shornuff, Jed!

The main mode of the long-distance trucker, especially one who drives alone, is loneliness.

Despite his rough-and-tumble reputation, the
lone truck driver needs to be introspective enough
faithful enough, hopeful enough, or just plain stupid
enough, to endure hours on end alone without going
insane. The cab of a truck is an isolation chamber. It
has pushed some to the extremes of human behavior. Or, maybe it just attracts people who tend to be
extreme in the first place. There have always been
stories of abductions and rapes. Drifters, whores,
and runaways had been found in shallow roadside
graves, hundreds of them over the years. A good
number of the perpetrators were found to be long-
distance truckers. This phenomenon was notable

enough to attract the special attention of the FBI, eventually. The investigators didn't speculate on whether serial killers became truckers because it gave them opportunities to practice their craft, or if the experience of being in a noisy, stressful and isolated environment for years on end pushed some otherwise normal men over the edge.

For Nick, driving was almost perfect in its own way. And Dr. Kultra had recognized it.

After listening to Nick's problems and history through several sessions, Dr. Kultra suggested that Nick take a job where he could concentrate on his own being for long periods to develop his awareness. Completely serious, without a drop of irony, the doctor suggested that Nick become a truck driver.

At first, Nick was flabbergasted. He had only recently learned to drive back then, having devoted most of his teen years to preparing for and then being in the army. Plus, his father had discouraged driving out of concern for Nick and his episodes. Nick had been somewhat fascinated with mechanical things as a child, but set most of those interests aside as adolescence approached, preferring instead to read books and play guitar. The idea of driving a truck hadn't occurred to him at all, and even if it had, he would have dismissed it as something he could have never tolerated for very long. Besides, who wanted to hang around truck stops? But then, this was a new reality, and as the doctor described what the job he had in mind would entail, Nick's interest grew.

He had been virtually unemployed at the time, sometimes working as a waiter or short-order cook. He was still bedeviled by the dead spot. Despite some early misgivings ("What if I blackout in the middle of a curve?") Dr. Kultra had convinced Nick that driving a truck would count as therapy and be profitable. In fact, he had already contacted a trucking company on Nick's behalf.

It was a simple yet demanding run going weekly from Chicago to L.A. and back along Steinbeck's "Mother Road," Route 66. He would have a two-day layover in L.A. among the palms and sunshine and then drive back the same way he came. The trucking company would pay all his expenses, and give him a comfortable salary. The whole arrangement promised the sort of soothing regularity that could help stabilize his mental processes, and would allow him to concentrate on his one imperative: awareness. After a few weeks of training and a single round-trip in the tutelage of an old-timer driver named Vern, Nick started on his long journey, traveling 2,250 miles over five days for each direction.

Hauling toilet paper. Or paper products. Or whatever.

Nick's anxiety had lessened over the years and miles. The dead spot had become a rarity. He had become far more self-aware, and for that, he thanked not only Dr. Kultra but also the hours he had spent in the cab of that Diamond T Model 921 tractor, listening to the Hall-Scott wailing along with the transmission in overdrive, occasionally downshifting a few gears to get around slower lines of trucks and cars as he blasted along.

As he drove, he would look at the Diamond-T logo in the center of the steering wheel, gazing into the center of it as though it were a mystical eye that held infinite truths. It was a blue diamond laid lengthwise, with a stylized *T* suspended in the center, cut in a strangely adorned typeface. It seemed out of place compared to the stolid block letters of the surrounding DIAMOND-T TRUCKS insignia, resembling a pair of mustaches or an old-style hypodermic or an archaic key of some kind. It almost looked Egyptian—an anachronism. It was as though the manufacturer had given Nick his own Rorschach to analyze or bedevil him while he drove this truck, a vehicle that was as much a product of Chicago as he was himself.

And what a truck it was. Gleaming red, with black and white pinstripes on the edge of the long hood and lining the borders of the cab and sleeper. Another logo projected out at the end of the hood, at the tip of the hood ornament, facing forward and mystically apprehending every mile's Dairy Queen, Foster's Freeze, Howard Johnson, Whiting, Sinclair, Standard, Texaco, and Brylcreem and Burma Shave ad, as well as all traffic he passed and all traffic that passed him going the opposite way. The T saw all. Maybe the "T" at the end of the hood was mystically linked through the ethers to the one in the middle of the steering wheel, and whatever was seen on the road was beamed directly into

Nick's skull. Maybe he didn't even need his own eyes to drive.

A deep chrome finish plated the air cleaner and the shell of the grill, as well as accents along the hood. Whenever he entered a truck stop after having the truck cleaned, other drivers—and even waitresses—would stop dead in their tracks to admire it.

"Whooo-weee, whatcha got there? Diamond T!"

"That's the Cadillac of trucks you got right there, boah."

"Ooooh! It's so pretty! All red and all. I want nail polish that color, Norma! I found my color!"

Nick warmly remembered the first time he saw his truck. He'd just taken his driver's training and tests in an old Mack A30 that had seen a few million miles and barely ran. It ran so badly that Nick had second thoughts about taking the job. Then, when he showed up at the Continental yard for his first solo run, his supervisor met him halfway across the parking lot. He was a short, fat Irishman they called Barry.

"OK, Pente, you know what this is?" He held up a shiny new key. "This is the key to your future happiness. It starts that truck right over there, which was just delivered yesterday. Treat that truck as you would your very own mother. In other words, don't fuck her up. Simple? Do yah got me?"

Sometimes while driving on sections of the freeways that were showing up here and there along his route, Nick would look down from the cab and see little boys gazing up from the cargo areas of their parents' station wagons, eyes wide with wonder at the enormous fire-engine red machine with dual chromed horns on top. They'd make little hand motions, and Nick would smile and oblige with a quick *doot doot* blast on the air horns. They would bounce with glee. It made him smile to make them smile. He was happy with the distance. He was happy with feeling like just another corpuscle in the bloodstream of America, aware of his own identity and satisfied to let other people have theirs, separated by distance and a couple panes of glass.

There were little rituals he enjoyed—things that made him feel he was part of the great drama of American ingenuity and dominance. At the times when his schedule was just right, he'd look off to the side of 66 as it left Victorville or Barstow and see the Santa Fe Super Chief running on the rails beside him--resplendent in its silver majesty. If traffic was light, he'd open up the throttle on his glorious machine and keep pace with the train, all the way up to one hundred miles per hour or more. The train's engineers would sometimes blow the horn for him, and he'd signal back with his own. Then, the road would curve or he'd start catching up with traffic and he'd lift and apply the brakes. Those were brief, magical moments in his life – a life rather dreary in many other ways.

He was alone, but he was aware. And he was comfortable. He was even "happy."

Or so he had thought.

Perhaps it was the outpouring of emotions with Euri or the realization that with her he wasn't really alone anymore or his sudden comprehension of the risks of *not* being alone that caused him to dream as he did that night. It seemed like a moment after he fell asleep, with Euri's head on his shoulder, he was back in the cab of his truck somewhere west of Albuquerque a few days earlier, where the infinite mesas offered views to distant horizons in every direction. Nick had beheld this same area almost two hundred times over the last five years, but never before had he been so fixated on his mirrors. And, this time, through the vibration of each, he could see the same black '55 Mercury coupe behind him at every mile. He would rev the truck hard to get around a line of cars, then would watch as the Mercury later made the same pass, sometimes dangerously. He was no longer alone on his route.

Nick looked down at the dashboard and realized that he was due another break, and that he needed more fuel. Even when he was cruising gently, the Hall-Scott veritably gulped gasoline, often returning not much more than three miles per gallon. The prospect of running out of gas while being tailed was anxiety he didn't need.

He saw a sign welcoming truckers and buses to an unnamed place in Acoma a few miles ahead. He pulled off the highway into the dirt lot of a truck stop that was called—simply-- "EAT." After carefully parking the truck where he could see it, he locked it and walked past some tables in front of the restaurant, which were gathered under fabric awnings. There was some real Indian jewelry on offer—but mainly plastic imitations. Toy dinosaurs glued to rocks for only a nickel. Real Indian blankets for only $1.99, possibly woven by a displaced tribe somewhere in Taiwan. An old Indian man sat at one of the tables and leaned back, a cowboy hat tipped down on his brow. A little girl stood at his side and looked at Nick suspiciously, never taking her eyes off of him as he walked past. He nodded and smiled at her. She didn't respond.

He looked around one last time before walking inside. No sign of any black Mercury.

Whereas the Jet had been the epitome of the modern and glamorous, EAT was no more than a Formica lunch counter with some booths. Circular fluorescent lights buzzed on the grease-stained ceiling. The menus were fly-specked. Almost everything appeared to be fly-specked, in fact, including the cake display. Not much had changed here since Steinbeck's Joad family ambled through in their '29 Hudson, fleeing the Dust Bowl. Nick took a booth this time—the better to keep an eye on the truck. Pat Boone echoed over the counter from a jukebox at the end of the room.

Nick stirred his coffee out of habit; he drank it black. This coffee was thick enough to resist the spoon. He lit a cigarette. As he sat and watched the clouds gather over the remains of a once-great civilization that called Acoma its "Sky City," he inevitably started listening in on a conversation in the booth across the aisle of the sparsely patronized diner.

"So then I told her...hehehe...I told her, I said, 'Settle down, now. Y'ain't got no reason to run. Pretty little thing like you ain't gon' be safe back at the truck stop!'"

His companion erupted in a high-pitched giggle that really didn't suit a fat man of about forty or so wearing bib overalls and a plaid shirt.

"*Safe!* Oh, Jed, that's rich. Safe! At the truck stop! Goddamn. This was in Little Rock?"

"Just outside. You know the hill? That one that ices over sometimes, y'know, just enough to slide and make ya wish ya had your chains on? Place to park on the side of the road? Yeah, it was that one. Little farm girl." More laughter. "Yeah," he continued. "I did get her back to the truck stop, eventually. Or somewhere close by, at least. I do hope things worked out for her. She couldn'ta been more than fourteen." Jed shrugged and shook his head, shaking off any responsibility.

"Sure aren't makin' 'em like they used to, Jed!" There was a deep, cackling guffaw.

"That's sure right. They don't even put up a real fight no more. Jesus." Jed shrugged. More laughs from the laughing man.

Jed appeared to be tall and gaunt with hollow cheeks. His eyes were caught in a perpetual sneer that gave the lie to any temporary curve of his lips. His cheeks were pockmarked, and before them was a sparse salt-and-pepper goatee. His head was topped with slicked-back dark hair that hadn't been washed in a while. The waitress, a thick girl of about eighteen wearing horn-rimmed glasses, came to their table. Both men went silent. Frank cleared his throat.

"Can I get you fellers some more coffee?" she asked, cheerfully.

Jed changed his tone to something softer and even more languorous than his usual drawl, with sounds that were drawn-out and laced with a bit of treacle.

"Yes, darlin'. Why doncha fill that cup up to the rim. We ain't going nowhere for a while." He smiled as he slowly placed his hand on her hip. As she filled the cup, Jed's eyes traced the outline of the pot and the cup silhouetted against her plump form, or that's what he wanted to seem to be doing. His head leaned back and chin turned up in a cocky way, eyelids suddenly heavy. Nick noticed the waitress's hands were shaking as she pulled away from Jed's outstretched hand, still tracing the side of her hip. She filled up both cups and walked away in a hurry.

"Whatcha thinkin', Jed?" asked his endomorphic pal.

Jed looked at him and sneered. He said slowly, pleadingly, "Now, if you need to ask, you *are* dumb as dog shit."

Howls of laughter. They died down only as the fat man pulled a pack of cigs out of the center pocket in his dirty overalls. Hard to light up while laughing.

"Y'know, Frank," he began, suddenly introspective. "There's just no tellin' about life and where it's gonna lead you."

"Shornuff, Jed!"

"Yep, I remember back when I got drafted. They weren't gon' take me at first because of my little problem with the Monroe County sheriff back then, but sure enough, they called me back a few weeks later and said, 'We seem to have lost your records,' or some bullshit. So, I went back in and filled out them forms the same way I done the first time, but I left off the part about jail. I figure what they don't know ain't gonna hurt 'em none. I think they knew it too."

"That's the truth!" said Frank, his blubbery lips pressing out something like a fart noise for emphasis. He laughed.

Jed's eyes tracked the girl as she served a piece of apple pie out of the fly-specked display case to an old man in a plaid shirt sitting at the counter and reading a newspaper. She was avoiding his gaze.

"And, you know," Jed continued. "If it hadn'ta been for that little change, I never would have gotten into the army back then, and I never would have started drivin' them deuce-and-a-halfs back then, and I wouldn'ta had my path in life that brought me here."

"Jed, you were truly fated and blessed by the Lord."

"I do believe it's so. Cuz drivin' trucks has taken me places I never thought I'd go," said Jed, obviously proud of the arc of his life.

"And all that pussy!" said Frank, his blubbering lips rattling off another raspberry. He shook his head in excitation, and his jowls flapped.

"Yes, and a lot of sweet, young pussy, too," said Jed. He pulled the cigarette from his mouth momentarily, and his tongue flicked out of his mouth and circulated around his lips, covering the chapped flesh between the opening of his mouth and his goatee. He leered at the girl behind the counter, now facing the kitchen order window with her back to him.

"But, ya know, Frank, there was times when I had my doubts. Y'know what I'm sayin'? There was that time I told you about back during the Red Ball Express days over in France. Remember that story? Shit, that guy..." Frank nodded, cigarette in his mouth. "I was runnin' ammo in that deuce from that port in Holland out to the lines in France, breakin' my balls, poppin' some reds now and then I got from a doctor in Havre. Y'know, just to keep goin'. Shit, they had me drivin' twenty-four hours a day sometimes.

"So, I come around this corner in the rain, haulin' some ass, just tryin' to stay on schedule. And goddamn if the front end don't start washin' out on me. What was I gonna do? Sure as shit, just in front of me, there's a couple infantrymen walkin' on the road just like this. So, this one...a private, I think... he sees my truck comin', and he just stands there. I mean, I can see his eyes and all, just over the hood of my truck. And then this sergeant tackles him and throws him out of the way, and my front end slams up against the rock wall. And so I sit in that truck just kinda dazed, and next thing ya know, I got this sergeant up in the cab, and he's holdin' his machine gun on me, callin' me all these names. Shit, it was an accident; any fool could see that. But he's holdin' this gun on me and callin' me a cunt and a cock-sucker and all, and I'm thinkin', hell, you're gonna get your fat fuck face thrown in the brig for actin' like that."

"Was he fat?" asked Frank, suddenly taking increased interest.

"Oh, hell yes. Redhead fat sonofabitch. I can still see his face lookin' at me. Thought I was 'bout ta die. I was just doin' my job. Can't account for no accidents all the time."

"Just doin' your job, Jed." Frank nodded in support.

Nick had stopped breathing. His gaze turned toward Jed, then quickly back to the tabletop in front of him. He remembered.

"Yep. So, ya never know where life is gonna lead ya, if ya know what I mean."

"Ain't that the truth," averred Frank, the remnants of a BBQ pork sandwich clinging to his left cheek. "Say, speaking of that, did you ever hear from that company about that sweet run down 66 like you was sayin'?"

Jed shook his head. "Y'know, for all the runnin' around they made me do, I shoulda been billin' 'em hourly. Buncha chicken shit, that's all it was. I don't know how they end up hirin' drivers. I called them, and they said they weren't hirin', but I left my number anyway. So, I get back to Tallahassee a few weeks later, and my wife's got a message. I call 'em, and they ask me all these questions goin' back to the war. I've never heard such a thing."

Frank shook his head in disbelief.

"But, then, get this. Gets even better. They want me to go to Chicago to this university and talk to someone. And I'm all...how's a feller supposta go from Florida to Chicago just for an interview for a drivin' job? It paid good, but not that good. And a university? Really?"

"Maybe it's papers for the university. Notes-papers, and such," offered Frank.

"I don't know what it was, but anyway, about a week later, I got a run scheduled for some orange juice up to Michigan, and I figure that's close enough. So, I went. I tell ya, Frank, if I could just settle into a single run workin' for a company, I'd give up this owner-operator shit right away. It's gettin' to be for the birds, 'specially with diesel gettin' to be more than a quarter a gallon. Shit.

"So, I go there to this university, and I see the guy, and he's this old German guy. A kraut. And he wants to talk to me about my childhood and the war and everything. Just for a drivin' job. And he's all, 'Well, this is really sensitive stuff, and we've had problems with drivers before, so that's why we screen 'em now.' He asks me if I ever done narcotics, and I say nah, just a little speed and some bennies durin' the war. And then he said, 'Will you take this spit test?' And I guess what they do is they put this thing on your tongue to see if you're on drugs and what all. And I'm like, no sir. Ain't gon' put nothin' on this old boy's tongue. So, he said thank you, and I never heard from him again."

"Just for a little speed?" Frank was aghast. "They ain't never heard of drivers takin' no speed?"

"I guess they was real serious about drugs and what all. Just for haulin' paper. Was a nice setup, though."

They both dwelled in a long silence. Jed continued to look at the girl, tracking her as she brought coffee and sandwiches to the other drivers who had filtered in to sit at the counter. She seemed to feel Jed's eyes on her. Jed appeared to enjoy her unease, to judge by the glint in his eyes and the occasional curl to his lips. In a minute or two, an older waitress came to Jed's table. She wore her skin like loose leather and had the drawl of the rocky deserts of west Texas.

"Boys, I'm takin' over this table from Jeanette. What can I get you?"

Jed looked up at her, his disappointment palpable. "Just the check please, ma'am." He and Frank looked at each other and pulled out their logbooks to enter their latest time. In a minute, they had left some coins on the table and were walking back to their trucks.

Nick sat at the booth and remembered that day on the road to Alsace. He remembered seeing the fast-approaching grill of a truck and the sound of tires sliding on wet pavement. He remembered someone shouting at him. Everything had seemed to shift into some ultra-sharp focus where he could even see the pitted metal on the truck's bumper and the lower half of the driver's face, his rotted teeth clenched and visible just over the steering wheel. Then, nothing. Nothing until the sound of Balsz going on for fifteen minutes as they walked along the road, reminding him about what a severely retarded dipshit he was, and how if he didn't pay attention, he was going to get them all killed.

"Did y'all want any ketchup?" He heard a voice, but it really didn't register. "Uh, sir." Nick glanced up. It was the plump girl, now back and holding a patty melt that was indifferently displayed on wilted lettuce, greasy thumbprints visible on the off-white china plate. Nick looked at the patty melt. He looked at it longer than he should have. He saw the ground beef, still leaking juice. And he saw the girl's face just behind it, smiling but getting more bewildered as seconds passed. He looked up at her, and his lips turned to a smile. She was a nice girl. The circular fluorescent light was directly above her head.

"Ketchup," he said, as if she had asked him if had wanted some enriched plutonium on the side. "No, no ketchup. Look, uh, miss, just give me the check, and I'll be on my way."

The girl was bewildered. "Oh, sir, I'm sorry. Did you want something else? You want this to go?"

"No, I just need to be going." Nick smiled, and the girl smiled back, shrugging as she took the plate back to the kitchen.

The total was $1.25, but Nick left two bucks. As he got up and walked out, a familiar song started playing on the jukebox. The older waitress had gone into conference with the plump one just in front of the order window.

As he walked out to the truck, there was still no sign of the black Mercury. As he unlocked the truck's door and stepped up into the cab, he noticed something in the side-view mirror as it swung around, showing him things behind his shoulder. Across the highway and to the side of a white-and-teal-colored mobile home, just barely visible from where he had parked, two men sat inside a black '55 Mercury. He climbed inside the truck and shut the door. He locked it.

He tried to make sense of what he had just heard. The "old German guy" at the university sounded all the world like Dr. Kultra, the man he credited with changing his life. How had he become part of the screening process for the trucking company where he had now worked for five years? In the time he was under the doctor's care, it seemed the man was just helping him out through a network of friends and acquaintances. Had it proven so successful that he had become an employee of Continental himself? And how strange it was that one of his prospective patients, or drivers, was likely the man behind the wheel of a truck that had nearly killed Nick thirteen years before.

Nick looked out the window at the mirror. He couldn't see the black Mercury, but the angle was different. It might have been there. It could be that they were just on the same trip as he was, going to L.A. It wasn't unusual for Nick to leave Chicago or L.A. and see cars and trucks he would later recognize along the way. Route 66 was like America's main drag, and even though it extended over two thousand miles, it seemed most drivers kept the same pace on their journeys in one direction or another. Aside from casual friendships at regular stops, it was as close to companionship as one usually got in this job.

"My name is Nick Pente. I am aware," he said quietly to himself.

He hadn't needed to do that in years.

There was another coping strategy Nick used in times of stress, and it was something he had recovered from a youth he had considered largely sad and wasted. He played guitar. His time on the road afforded opportunities to sit in the sleeper cab behind him and slightly restore himself by doing something he had come to consider true recreation. And when he was feeling washed out and dissolute, it was usually time to pull over for the night or at least a few hours and play on his Gibson archtop. At times, he'd play songs. Other times, he'd just play scales, or he'd go on for a few minutes improvising on some little snippet of a scale that had come to him while driving, perhaps mimicking the sound of the whining gears or the rattle of the cab over rough stretches of road. Most of it didn't make any sense, but it seemed to pull Nick back together after being stretched thin. So, he sat in back of the sleeper, picked up his worn Gibson and started to plunk out chords. After a while, a song had started to come to him. He tried to remember the words to the song. But he didn't sing. He didn't consider himself a singer.

After an hour or so, he figured he had better get moving. He craned his neck to look at the spot beside the mobile home across 66. The Mercury had gone.

But it would be back.

7

The Loom

*N*ick awakened to the sound of chanting.

It was Bacho, but he sounded different than before, back when Nick was being dragged along the ground in the litter. This time, it was in a higher register and slower, with each note more sustained than before. He started to feel tapping on each knee. It smarted. Slowly, and with some trepidation, he opened his eyes.

Over Nick stood a masked figure. The mask made the figure look like an oversized tar baby with a span of feathers rising up behind it. It was red and white and orange and turquoise. The figure bounced and nodded slowly as Bacho's voice rang out. Nick's eyes widened.

Then, Euri's face appeared in the foreground. She was interposing herself between him and the dancing figure in the middle of the hut.

"Nick, it's my father. He's going to fix your legs."

The wailing, dancing, and nodding went on in the background, just over her head. She had said what she said in a way that was somehow domestic. It was like, "Honey, Dad is here. He's going to help you with the mower." It was so normal -- its plain, quotidian nature -- and in such contrast to the scene visible just over Euri's shoulder that Nick didn't know if he found in it reassurance, or evidence he was just terminally confused.

Nick watched the bouncing head and the body covered in pelts and feathers and beads. Bacho kicked his legs as he went on wailing, making the shack tremble. He shook a feathered staff. Nick looked down at his own knees in bed. His legs were intact but showed burn marks beneath a white glaze resembling a salve. The feeling of the cold air on them -- and the occasional mild slap of Bacho's staff -- somehow reassured him. He could twitch his feet, even though his legs wouldn't respond when he tried to lift them.

Bacho's song came to a crescendo. He lifted the staff above his mask and held it high. He was silent for only a few dramatic seconds, then said something in his native tongue. Euri responded, then turned to Nick.

"He says you can sit up now."

Nick looked at her, skeptically. He tried moving his legs. Nothing.

"Come, try to sit," said Euri. Bacho looked on. Gently, Nick took Euri's hand.

Nick tried to remember what it felt like to have legs. Legs that worked. He tried to think of sending a signal from his brain down his spinal column to some receptors in his thighs. He tried to move. Nothing.

Then he looked at Bacho, standing in the middle of the hut just over the trap door that concealed Euri's library, and he thought he wasn't the one to move his legs. His legs would move on their own. There was no quasi-mechanical action he could take that would cause a chain of electrical and chemical events. His legs would move, if they could.

His knee moved. Then it moved more toward the edge of the bed. The other knee followed. Shaking now, but still moving, it cleared the edge of the mattress. His left calf fell toward the floor. Euri took his other hand and pulled, and in a moment he was upright for the first time in what felt like an eternity. He sat on the edge of the bed. He could feel his legs, and he could feel the bottoms of his feet touch the floor. Euri smiled at him and squeezed his hand. He smiled back.

"Now, stand," she said. Bacho's mask nodded. Nick heard a brief grunt resonating from somewhere inside.

Nick felt pressure on the soles of his feet. Euri moved in front of him and took both of his hands.

Nick felt some inner motivation taking over. He wasn't entirely conscious of it. He leaned forward. He gazed at Bacho's mask. Bacho shook his staff.

He felt lifted, and in a moment, he was on his feet before Bacho.

Bacho's hands rose to his mask and lifted. Then was revealed the exact face that Nick had imagined when Bacho had told him there were more ways to see than with his eyes. A tall, stoic, native man of about seventy -- his skin weathered, his eyes deep, his hair more salt than pepper. An old Indian guy. An old Indian guy slowly smiling. He had the same saffron-brown eyes of his daughter. His skin was a bit darker than hers. He raised his hands in an apparent blessing and placed them on Nick's shoulders. He shook his head and grunted.

Euri stood smiling, grasping her hands and bouncing with delight.

Nick moved around, but felt unsteady. He had a tingling down the back of his left thigh, ending in his heel somewhere. His gut was still sore. His driver's uniform had been replaced by a poncho. He noticed his clothes had been removed, though he still wore his underwear. Tighty-whities, to be exact. Absent-mindedly, Nick lifted the poncho to see what was underneath. Euri shyly turned away.

"Hey, Nick," said Bacho. "It still cold outside. Cold in here too." Nick quickly dropped the poncho to cover himself, blushing. Euri giggled.

"Bacho," he began, gathering his senses to help him seem more earnest. "I want to thank you and

Euri for your hospitality and your care for me. I still don't really know what's going on, but I feel welcomed here as your guest. I want to thank you for that, and I want to thank you for whatever you just did that allowed me to walk again. I don't know what to say or how to repay you, but when I get back to Seligman, I'm going to..." He looked at Euri. She demurely turned away.

Bacho looked him in the eye, then looked at Euri. "You talk to Euri. I get soup. More soup." He turned to walk out of the hut, then stopped. "And, uh, you clean. Wash up. You still got, uh, stuff. Euri, you show the man." Bacho walked out, gently shutting the door behind him.

Euri and Nick were alone. It wasn't the first time, but it felt like something new. He was seeing her for the first time when not feeling like an invalid in her care. Something came over him. He didn't quite know how to interpret it. Euri was shy but coping with it well. It appeared she was avoiding him. Nick moved around, slowly. It was painful. He felt weak. His whole body was sore. He felt the freshness of burns on his legs. Really, he was just delighted to be standing and walking. He staggered. He felt dizzy. Euri moved to brace him and helped him sit down on the edge of the bed.

"It's a miracle. A real miracle. Your father cured me!" he said, finally looking down at his poncho and legs. "I should be driving again in no time. I'm still a little weak, maybe, but—"

"Well." Euri seemed charmed, maybe a little too much. "Well, actually, I think it was a pinched nerve in your lumbar area. Maybe from when you got that bruise on your belly. I think it was sleep and rest that made you better."

Nick stopped breathing for a second. The way she pronounced "lumbar" as "*loom*-bar," she could have been an osteopath. She could tell he was taken aback.

"See?" she said, pulling back her blanket on her bed to reveal a thick book called *Manual Medicine* by E.J. Hawthorne. It had the name "Stewart" etched in pencil along the side.

"Who is 'Stewart?" asked Nick.

"I don't know. My father got it for me."

Nick was overwhelmed by emotions he didn't know how to express. He slowly got to his feet again and moved toward her, looking into her panicked eyes while smiling. She shook nervously and set the book down on her bed. She moved toward the door. "I'll get you some water...for washing."

Nick gently sat down on the bed yet again. He heard Euri fluttering about outside, talking to Bacho in their native language. He took this opportunity to take stock. He was in a drafty shack on a mountain, probably not far from Seligman. Somehow, he was saved from almost certain death back on the bridge. Aside from some bruises, burns, and soreness, he felt fine. What's more, he felt for the first time -- perhaps the first time ever -- he was in love. He was in love with no less than a young Indian maiden who had grown up alone with her father in that very same shack. Somewhere in the back of his mind were foggy memories of the truck, the secret "paper product" load, the trucking company, Dr. Kultra, the two men and what they said and did. But all of that now seemed as distant and inconsequential as the little shacks he had seen at a distance from Route 66 hundreds of times before. They had been the ones that made him occasionally, briefly wonder how it was that anyone could live that way and what animals they must be. It seemed for years he had lived inside of himself, dwelling inside the truck and never daring to look very far outside of it. Now, he had escaped in a manner that could only be described as explosive. He looked around the shack. Things seemed clearer to him. Not as clear as they did during the times when the dead spot took him. No, this was the clarity he had been striving for, something he knew could be there behind the fog and the fear and all the artifice he took on to counteract the fog and fear. He could see the grains in the wooden slats, the cobweb in the corner, the rough way that "Stewart" had been drawn in capital letters on the side of the textbook, the low flame inside of the potbelly stove, the sawdust and scraps on the floor around it, more cobwebs in the corners of the mica-paned windows, the dusty sheepskin covering the loom. He lifted his hands and looked at them in front of the scene in the room around him. They were his hands. The callouses from the guitar. The cuticles. The dirt beneath the nails. A gash or two on his palms. Scabs on his knuckles. He was here, and he was aware.

For the first time in longer than he could remember, he was actually curious about something. He was curious because he wanted to know, not because he needed to know for his job or his survival.

Nick looked at the loom in front of him. Curiosity drew him across the room. He got up again, this time with only a little difficulty, and haltingly walked toward it. The dusty sheepskin covered almost all of the rug on the loom beneath. He bent at the waist to lift it. The door squeaked open.

"Don't!" gasped Euri. Nick straightened and stepped back. Euri rushed in with a bowl of hot water, sloshing it in her haste. "He doesn't want anyone to see that! Never touch that! *Never!*" Her last word was spoken almost in a growl. Her eyes were aflame. Her lips pursed and trembled in alarm and urgency.

Nick gulped, embarrassed. He had been nosy. "I'm very sorry," he said. She caught her breath and set the bowl down on a stool. She set a few rough cloths next to it.

"You can wash with this. Then, come outside." She looked at him and slowly a little smile came back to her lips. She turned to walk outside, but before she left, she turned back to face him, preparing to speak.

"I won't touch the loom," Nick said.

"Thank you."

8

Sliding Ninths

*N*ick washed his face as best he could with the small pieces of cloth and the once-hot, now-lukewarm water in the bowl.

Then, he remembered he wasn't wearing pants.

They hadn't gone far, he hoped. Scrounging around he chanced to turn over the pillow in the crude bed and found the navy blue pants and red shirt of his driver's uniform folded and hung over the primitive headboard. They looked like they had been washed. The legs of the pants had been mended with rough thread, and the holes that remained showed where the burn marks on the fronts of his thighs and shins had come from. He didn't clearly remember the event that caused them. He only remembered falling into the path of the train, those perilous last moments before all turned white. He carefully slipped back into the pants, pulled on his black wool socks (also washed), put on his still shiny, nonskid, oil-resistant, nonmarking shoes, then pulled the poncho back over his head. The air remained cold.

The thick and yellowed windowpanes prevented him from seeing anything going on outside in detail, but he could see colored shapes and figures moving around occasionally. It was in the late afternoon, just as the shadows were lengthening. He opened the door on a scene from a postcard: Bacho and Euri sitting around a campfire near a crude sheep pen, and the long stratocumulus clouds sparsely towering over the grassy valley. The clouds took on a reddish tint at their edges. He stood at the doorway of the shack and gazed into what seemed like forever. A flock of sheep *baahed* softly in the background. An old bay horse foraged in the field.

Bacho turned and nodded. Euri had already been watching the door, waiting for Nick. With a bounce, she stood and smiled.

"Come over. Warm by fire," said Bacho. Nick slowly, almost creakingly, walked over to the fire where two pots were suspended and some sort of cast-iron box sat in the center. Bacho pointed to a portion of a stump, and Nick slowly took his seat, his legs still throbbing.

The farm lay in a meadow in the middle of a valley. There were peaks on either side, and a light dusting of snow covered their summits. The tree line ended not far above the valley floor, so Nick assumed they had to be fairly high up already, maybe close to seven thousand feet or so. Nick could see no road, and the paths leading to and from the farm were only wide enough for a man or a horse.

Bacho offered him more of the mutton stew that had proven so restorative before. He dished it out of the cast iron pot over the fire. Nick nodded in thanks.

"I don't suppose I could trouble you for a cup of coffee and a cigarette, could I?" asked Nick. Bacho looked at him, blankly. Euri translated. Bacho's face lit up with sudden recognition.

"No! No coffee and no..." he made a hand gesture of smoking a cig. "Don't have that here. Only sheep." He laughed, showing a full complement of mildly-yellowed teeth. Euri laughed. The sheep were slightly yellowed as well.

Then, there was silence. It was a silence that seemed like it should have been awkward, but it really wasn't. Nick was just at a loss of what to say. "Nice place you've got here." "Weather's fine." "What's the name of that sheep?" "Your daughter is very beautiful." Given all that had happened in the time he had been on the farm, nothing seemed the right thing to say. He didn't even know how long it had been. He didn't know what day it was. He knew the truck had crashed on a Thursday. It had been his third-going-on-fourth day out of Chicago. He tried to count the number of times he had awakened since and tried to remember if he had seen daylight each time. It could have been the same day as his arrival. The burns on his legs still felt fresh, but not that fresh. He wondered if they had been worse at one time, and how much worse. He noticed something in his pants pocket. He reached in to find his Hamilton watch. It was cracked and had stopped at around 5:20 a.m. on November 14, the morning of the crash. He noticed that his right hand had scabs on it. He couldn't quite remember how they got there. Nothing around him told him how much time had passed. He thought that would be as good a place to start as any. He finally had a question. But, then, in the back of his mind, he sensed he knew what the answer would be.

"What day is it?"

Bacho and Euri looked at him.

"Today. This day. It's near the low sun. Not long now." Bacho looked back to the fire, stirring some embers with a long stick. He was sincere.

"Well, do you have a calendar or anything?"

"You got to go? Somewhere?"

"Well, no."

"Then..."

"Yes, '*Why is it important?*' That's the next question. I know." He was frustrated. Euri and Bacho looked at him. Nick felt his brow furrow. He took a deep breath. He looked around. He tried to think of what he had been missing and what he still missed. Coffee would be nice. A cigarette would be nice. But did he need either? No shakes, no twitchiness. No physical signs of withdrawal. He just felt more comfortable with a hot cup of black fluid in one hand and a burning stick in another, as he had for most of the preceding twenty years. He took another deep breath.

"I'm sorry."

"You miss your home?" asked Euri, gently.

"No. Not really," answered Nick after a pause, summoning an honesty borne out of slight introspection. "I don't really have much of a home right now. I just drive, mainly. I live in my truck. But it's important I get back there. I need to know—"

"Your truck gone," said Bacho, imitating an explosion with his hands and pushing out his lips in a sort of pout. He still stirred the embers, staring at them.

"Yes, I know. At least, I think I know. I don't remember much about what happened." Nick suddenly stumbled on a question. "Say, how did you save me? How did you pull me from that wreck? I don't remember anything after falling. I was hanging one moment, and then the train came."

"I was down there for a while, and I was coming back. I see you hanging there. So, I got you out."

"But how?"

"I pull."

"Just you?" Bacho didn't understand. Euri said something to him.

"Just me. Hehehe. Old Indian guy." There was a pride in his smile.

"No one was around? No cops? Police?"

"Oh, no police. No sheriff. Just two guys. White guys."

Nick froze. His eyes widened.

"These two guys; what did they look like?"

"They don't look too good."

"I mean, can you describe them?"

"One tall, one short. They don't look too good. So, I bring you here."

"Did they chase you?"

"Chase? No. I didn't see. I just walk. I put you on my blanket. Travois. See?" Bacho pointed to a blanket strung with leather straps between two long poles with worn ends. It was leaning against the shack.

"Well, thank you," It was all Nick could think to say at that moment. He looked down at his knuckles.

Euri seemed to want to change the subject. "Nick, you live in your truck?" Her eyes showed concern, as if she couldn't imagine how that would be possible, and that she felt sorry for him if it was so.

"Well, not really. I mean -- I have an address. I live in Chicago. It's where I'm from. When I go to L.A., I stay in a hotel, and then I go back to Chicago.

"Chi-ca-go?" She pronounced each syllable clearly. "The big town? Do they have many books?"

"Oh, yes! Many, many books. And theaters and museums and cars and airplanes. It's hog butcher to the world! Tool maker! Stacker of wheat! That's what the poet said. Do you know that poem?" Euri was excited but just shook her head. Never before had Chicago seemed so exciting, so bracing as it did when Nick saw it through her eyes. He felt he hadn't been so excited about anything in years.

"You live there? In Chicago?"

"Well, I have a place there. An apartment."

"You have wife there, too?" asked Euri.

"No, no wife. I would never be able to see her if I did."

Euri and Bacho looked at each other. Euri then started talking to her dad in English, explaining something about Nick and recalling his earlier conversation with him, but it soon trailed off into her native dialect. At the end, Bacho's back gently slumped. He shrugged. He seemed at a loss for words. He turned to Nick.

"You alone too much."

"Oh, I'm never really alone. I kind of, you know, read magazines, and I play guitar a little. When I'm in Chicago there are all sorts of things to do. Nightclubs, TV, bars. All kinds of things."

Bacho only nodded. Euri looked at him, concerned. "You alone too much," he said, again. "Better here." Euri's gaze turned to Nick.

"It might seem that way," continued Nick, "but really, there's so much going on that you just don't feel alone. Always new people to meet. Always noise and things, and we have things that you never dreamt of. We have TV. We have restaurants. We have stores. And, just last weekend, I..." Nick looked at Bacho. He wasn't buying it. Euri got up from the fire with a little nod.

"Your people, where they from?" asked Bacho.

"You mean my nationality? Like my forefathers? They're Greek -- from Greece. My mother was Irish." There was a look of recognition on Bacho's face.

"Greek! Euri name Greek. That not Indian name, not Hopi or Navajo. I don't know what means. Mother name her. Mother was from school. She learn that there. I'm just old Indian guy. 'Euri-dee-chay.'" Bacho brokenly pronounced it and shrugged. Nick just smiled and nodded. He didn't recognize the name as Greek when pronounced that way. Most of his female relatives on his dad's side were called Mary or Sophia or Margaret. His family didn't stay close to tradition much.

"I am Bacho. Bacho mean coyote in Apache. Dog who runs. Steal sometime. Do crazy thing. But he not bad. Hehehe." Bacho smiled and nodded as he chuckled. "And your name, what mean?" Nick couldn't think of what "Nicholas" meant. He thought he remembered seeing it in one of those baby-name books once. He thought he recalled it meaning "protector" or "victor" or something. But then it seemed that every male name meant "protector" or "victor." These were things parents wanted their boys to be like. However, he did know something about his last name.

"My last name is Pente. It's a shortened form of 'Pentangeloi.' We...my father's people, shortened it when they came through Ellis Island. So, now it's just 'Pente.' It used to mean 'five angels,' but now it just means 'five' in its short form. Kinda funny. I'm 'Nick Five.'" He smiled and chuckled, somewhat embarrassed. There was silence. Bacho just gazed at him, then went back to looking at the fire. He grunted.

Nick sensed something next to him. He looked up and was amazed. Euri was holding his guitar, the one he had last known to exist as it pressed into the back of his head while he was hanging in the truck, about to crash into the train. She handed it to him, positively beaming and doing a shy little modified curtsey. He was astonished.

"This is your guitar? You play?"

Nick took the tobacco and orange-colored Gibson archtop and gazed at it like an old friend, which it was. Probably the only friend he had left from his old life. He noticed the places on the back where his belt buckle had gouged the wood. Could he be dreaming this? If so, it would be the first dream he had where his feet felt too warm against the fire, and he could smell the remnants of mutton burning off in the flames.

Nick set the guitar on his knee. He strummed -- just a few chords. High E was flat. He fixed it. Euri looked on in excited adoration. Bacho grunted.

"How did you get this out of my truck?" asked Nick, though he was no more hopeful of an informative response than he was in regards to any other question.

"I pull," said Bacho.

And now, the music flowed. Nick played a nice little comping arrangement of "Slow Boat to China," then slid into an instrumental of "All of Me." He looked around him, at the sheep he was serenading, the mountains, the clouds, and the setting sun. The stars were gradually appearing more dense in the night sky. He felt that he belonged. Through some weird labyrinth of fate that no one dare try to explain, he was here. He would need to surrender to his circumstances and accept that he, Nick Pente, orphaned son of a Greek optician and a drunken Irishwoman, loner scion of Chicago, wounded veteran of the Battle of the Bulge, victim of an apparent neuropathic disorder, failed student, adequate guitarist, and, until recently, a successful long-haul truck driver, was here in a remote sheep farm somewhere in northern Arizona, attended to by an old Indian guy and his beautiful and surprisingly-educated daughter, playing jazz guitar on a stump to an audience of sheep (mainly). And he had to know that it was where he belonged right then.

He was aware.

The last notes of the song trailed off into tinkling suspended fourths and diminished ninths, and Euri looked at him, beaming. Bacho smiled from the corner of his mouth and grunted.

"Do you sing?" asked Euri. "Sing a song!"

Nick had never really tried to sing. It wasn't his thing. Actually, singing had nearly brought on an early episode of the dead spot on a couple of occasions when he was a kid, back in middle school, whenever he was expected to sing the national anthem or "America the Beautiful." He coped by just mouthing the words and hoping the loud, atonal nasally chirp of Becky Permentier at the next desk over covered for him. He had hoped he'd be over that fear by now, but old habits and fears die hard. He grimaced. Euri's eyes pleaded with him. He surrendered, yet again.

But what to sing? Nick searched his memory. Nothing came to mind. Then, somewhere out of the depths of came something he had been unable to escape for months on end. He had heard it at every jukebox at every stop—on occasion, multiple times. He tried to remember the chords, strumming to get the right key. The chords were easy, plain old one/four/five and back to one. Oldest one in the book. Corny. He cleared his throat and began:

> *Find a wheel and it goes round, round, round,*
> *As it skims along with a happy sound!*
> *As it goes along the ground, ground, ground--*
> *Till it leads you to the one you love!*
> *Then your love will hold you round, round, round,*
> *In your heart's a song with a brand new sound!*
> *And your head goes spinning round, round, round,*
> *'Cause you've found what you've been dreamin' of!*

And then he paused to remember the bridge:

> *In the night you see the oval moon*
> *Going round and round in tune*
> *And the ball of sun in the day*
> *Makes a girl and boy wanna say.*

His voice cracked on that last high note. Perry Como, he wasn't. He wasn't even Jimmy Durante. He coughed, shook his head, and continued:

Find a ring and put it round, round, round
And with ties so strong that two hearts are bound
Put it on the one you've found, found, found
For you know that this is really love.

As he ended, he found himself looking into Euri's eyes, and her sweet, innocent round-eye expression staring back at him. Something was welling up in his throat and making his head warm. He stopped playing. It was almost like the dead spot was coming back, but not really. His hands felt funny, but not really, not in the same way they did all the times before. Still, he looked at Euri. Her chest rose with each deep breath. She touched him, letting her hand rest on his forearm. "Play it again!" she said.

Bacho grunted. "Good song," he said. He went back to stirring the embers with a stick. "Perry Como," he grunted.

After a few more verses of Perry's hit, Nick's voice started to go hoarse. Bacho and Euri smiled at each other and soon retired to the shack, leaving Nick with his guitar at the fire. Nick felt some new energy coming into his fingers and kept playing, pausing only to wish Euri a good night. He tried not to look at her. His face felt strange. He kept playing. It was a joy to play there under the stars.

As he struck a few sliding ninths, he tried to remember where he had heard them before. Those were the chords to the song playing on a jukebox or something similar the last time he heard recorded music.

He heard music in Flagstaff, after the long drive from Acoma along Route 66. The road out of New Mexico had taken him through Grants and Gallup, through the Petrified Forest, where the dry and desolate rocks suddenly got more colorful, through the rolling hills and vast mesas near Saunders, Holbrook and Winslow, all bordering on Navajo land, past the landmarks of the ancient Meteor Crater and the road to the slightly-less-ancient cliff dwellings of Walnut Canyon, and up a sharp rise past Winona and into the railway town of Flagstaff. And all that way in the fading light behind him, there was a black dot always somewhere, weaving in and out of traffic, pacing him from a safe distance. Nick tried to put it out of his mind. He tried to let it slide.

It was time to stop again. For the first time since Amarillo, Nick had a place in mind: The world-famous Heartland Resort.

The Heartland was almost a destination in itself. It had a full-service hotel, an extensive miniature golf course, an indoor pool, and a giant twenty-four-hour coffee shop that served things no other place did for hundreds of miles in either direction along 66 -- though Nick never chose those items off the menu. When Nick would leave L.A. on his return trip, it was always The Heartland he was aiming for at the end of the first day's travel. It presented itself as a sort of compendium of everything America could offer the world in this part of the twentieth century—all pleasantly gathered together in a modern glass-walled building on a multi-acre site in Flagstaff. It was an embassy and museum of sorts. It was a Harvey House for the new international era.

The only trouble with it this time was that he would need to park his truck across the road from the dining room, and he might not be able to see it as well as he'd like. When he hit the kill switch and the Hall-Scott stopped with a *chuff*, he sat and thought as the exhausts cooled with their familiar ticking sound. From where he was parked, he could see people in the booths through the restaurant windows. He stared down at the key in the ignition. Restarting the truck, he re-parked it with the rear doors facing the restaurant. With the maneuver complete, he locked up the truck, lit a cig, and strode through the cold night air across the lot and access road. There was no sign of a black Mercury.

He entered through the large A-frame lobby with the angular, multi-colored, Mondrian-like windows over the door. They were the modern take on stained glass in this cathedral, itself another stop on a pilgrimage along a holy path. Bison greeted him on either side of the doors, on the roof, and even in the foyer. They weren't real bison. They were only fiberglass. The Heartland had taken the bison as their mascot. Nothing said "heartland" better than buffalo, never mind that they had been hunted almost to extinction. At least they still had nice fiberglass replicas. Most of them had long eyelashes and, in some faint way, smiles.

A version of "Mr. Sandman" played on muted trombone wafted through the smoky air as Nick approached the hostess station. He looked into the dining room, and then back through the lobby doors he had just entered. He was searching for any sign of the two men. The hostess, a plump-faced, stout blond woman of about forty, approached him with a place setting and a menu.

Nick smiled. "Just waiting on a couple friends, thanks." She smiled and turned back to her side work in the beverage area.

Nick could just barely see the gas pups through the lobby doors. No sign of the Mercury. Other parties trickled in. The hostess was quick to seat them. Some were truckers. Some looked like families on vacation, with dad, mom, and the kids in the latest casual wardrobe from a Sears catalogue. A few young soldiers wandered up and were promptly seated by the hostess with a smile and cheery small talk. A rumple-suited salesman with a sample case was escorted to a table.

A few more parties were seated and the warm air started to carry the aroma of brown gravy and warm, buttery rolls, Nick noticed a man standing to the side of the hostess podium. He was tucked back in the passageway that led past the payphones and to the restrooms. He was young and wore a light blue windbreaker, his hair in a close Afro. Whenever the hostess would return to seat another party, he would look at her expectantly, like he wanted to say something. One time, he even raised his finger tentatively, but then after the hostess obviously ignored it, almost pushing it out of the way as she seated an older white couple in ranch-wear, the young man let it wilt back down until it found its home in the pocket of his windbreaker.

Nick looked at the crowd in the restaurant again. Everyone seated at the tables and booths had one thing in common.

He had seen this sort of thing at various places throughout his travels. He never got into the deep South on his route, so any cases of out-and-out separatism were occasional and rather surprising. Chicago had its race issues back then, but skin color didn't exclude anyone from at least getting a table at a restaurant -- not in the places Nick frequented, at least. If it hadn't quite yet fully embraced its black culture, Chicago in the 1950s had at least acqui-esced to the fact that money in black hands had the same value as it did in white ones.

Nick had spent enough time and care on the Mercury men. Anyway, the scent of chicken-fried steak and roast beef were drawing him within. He sauntered to the hostess station, making eye contact and nodding at the young black man to his right. The young man nodded politely, the strain of tension in his eyes.

As Nick reached the podium, an elderly woman wearing a hat entered from the lobby and stood behind him. She was a white lady of about seventy, wearing a net veil that almost covered her face. Her name was probably Gladys. She wore a stole, its little dehydrated fox head resting just off her right side. She looked up at the young black man, who was about a foot taller than she.

"*Boy*, we need a table for three. Can you hurry, please, *boy*?"

"Uh, I'm sorry, ma'am. I don't work here." His voice was low and soft, and he took on a deferential smile, nodding his head in a way that made it seem like he'd been practicing the gesture throughout his twenty-five or so years.

"Oh, then how do we get a table? Are you uh…" The woman was confused.

Just then, the hostess strode back from seating the last party. "Hello, and welcome to The Heartland! Thank you for joining us this evening. How many in your party? Four?" she said to Nick. He realized she thought he was with Gladys and the two other old women. Nick looked at the black man, briefly making eye contact again. The black man's eyes shifted away nervously.

Nick cleared his throat. "Oh, sorry, I'm not with them. I need a booth for two, please. Can you get us something close to the front windows? I need to keep an eye on my truck. Here, this is the one I was waiting on." He gestured to the black man, then turned his head to him and offered a quick wink.

The hostess suddenly went, if not cold, then lukewarm. She looked into Nick's eyes, and, for the first time, in the direction of the young black man. She had been bending down to pick up a menu, and now, half-frozen in that position, she looked at both of them again.

"Miss? Miss?" said Gladys (or whatever her name was) from behind Nick. "Could we get a table, please? My friend Edna has low blood sugar!"

The hostess looked back at Nick. Her face bore the expression of having been bettered at a game she wished she didn't have to play.

"Certainly, sir," she said coldly, picking up another menu and place setting. She turned and started walking stiffly toward the dining room. Nick followed her. He sensed the young black man had been caught entirely off guard. He stood in the passageway, his gaze bouncing back and forth between Nick and the hostess. Nick looked at him and subtly waved, his hand below his beltline. The black man followed him, self-consciousness oozing with every step. They were seated together at a booth on the far end of the restaurant, in a section that was nearly vacant. Nick didn't mind; it happened to give him the best view of the back end of the trailer in the lot across the street.

Nick looked across at the young black man, who was still surveying him nervously.

"You aren't from around here, are you?" he finally asked Nick.

"No. Chicago. I'm Nick Pente." he extended his hand.

"Shelby. Shelby Howell." The man shook his hand. "Look," he said, "I'm not looking for any handout. I got my own money and all. I just don't have a car right now. Look out the window. You see over there? See that white car, the old Buick? That's mine. It blew a radiator hose, and all the shops are closed. So, I gotta stay here for the night. I'll probably sleep in my car. But I was looking for a place to sit and get something to eat, and it seems that—"

"I know, I know. Not used to seeing that. OK, no handout offered. Just figured I could help you out, and I'm usually looking for good conversation. Hope that's OK with you."

Shelby finally exhaled. He smiled and then shook his head in disbelief at what he had gone through to get the chance to buy a club sandwich and a Coke.

"Yeah, L.A. isn't like this. In most places, at least. Just gotta know the right parts of town."

"That where you're from?"

"Yeah, L.A. Long Beach. You know that part?"

"I don't get down there much. My run ends in Pomona. I usually get a hotel around there."

Shelby showed some sudden interest. "Pomona, huh?"

The waitress took their orders in silence and with some impatience. The conversation continued. Nick learned that Shelby had been in the army as well, serving a couple years in Korea. After his discharge, he worked odd jobs as a cook or a cleaner or longshoremen's assistant. His parents threw him out after he got his girlfriend pregnant about a year back. Things had been hard since, but he was headed somewhere back East to stay with a cousin who offered him work and a place to live. Nick listened without judgment. He surmised the kid had skipped out on the girl and the baby. He had heard far, far worse.

It was at some point halfway through Nick's chicken-fried steak with mashed potatoes that something compelled Shelby to say, "But I thank God Almighty that I don't use dope. Lotta people do out there in the world today."

"I know," said Nick, casually. He gathered that Shelby felt a need to dispel some assumptions white people usually made about black people. Nick let him.

"Yep, and it's just gettin' worse. I saw what it did to guys in Korea, and after. Guys shooting up with heroin -- sometimes mixed with speed. Sometimes, they'd go out there and just not give a care -- walk right into a tank. I lost, like, five buddies out of my company because they OD'd. And the Chinese, they all seemed to be on something when we'd take them as prisoners. Everybody on both sides just tryin' to shut off the world. So, some of the GIs brought all that back with them now. Some of them were doing it just to get an early discharge. They're all like, 'Yeah, I use drugs. Send me home!' Better than this, dishonorable discharge or not. So, they all come back here." He lit a cigarette.

"So, now what it's doing to my old neighborhood is even worse. Junkies in the streets. We always had 'em. Drunks too. Usually the drunks was more common than the junkies and the hopheads and pill poppers and whatever. There's just a lot more of everything now. Especially the dope fiends."

"I can imagine," said Nick, shaking his head. He only used alcohol and the occasional brothel visit to shut the world off during his time in the war.

"But, y'know, recently something really weird, strange, has been happening," Shelby continued while absently twirling a sugar packet on the table. "There's these paddy-wagon-type things that come down through the neighborhood. Usually white guys driving them. They pick up the winos and hopheads and junkies, and they say they're taking them to this place in Pomona. They say they're doing some sort of treatment on them to help them out. That's why I was interested when you said Pomona."

"Oh, I just drop off my load there and go back to Chicago. Usually, I'm empty on the way back. I don't know much about Pomona. Seems OK." Nick noticed various people at the tables and booths and even counter turning around to look at the two of them. Some would shake their heads in disbelief, then turn back to their conversations.

"So, what are you carrying?"

"Paper products. Toilet paper, supposedly."

Shelby glared at him. He shook his head, disbelievingly. "They pay you to drive a truck full of *toilet paper* from Chicago to L.A., then go back empty?"

He said this slowly, with each syllable softly conveying a sense of utter bullshit.

"Well, yeah, for the last five years. It's their money. I don't know that it's toilet paper, exactly. The manifest says 'paper products.' Could be anything, really. Any paper product." Nick shrugged.

"Money. Money's paper," said Shelby, his eyebrows flexing slightly.

"I really don't think it's money," said Nick, a little nervously, but just a little. "They don't give me any police escort or anything. Anyway, I would have found out by now if it was, and I'd—"

"You'd be gone. Right, man? Havana." Shelby smirked, taking a swig of Coke.

"Well, someone would be gone. Maybe not me."

"So, you ain't really curious about what it really is?" asked Shelby.

"Hey, they're paying me. I really don't care. As long as the load doesn't kill me," said Nick, feeling pressured.

"Or, someone maybe decides...never mind." Shelby shook his head again. "I just can't believe you never opened it up and looked at what they got you carrying. I mean, just out of curiosity. Could be explosives. They can lie on a manifest. Did it at the docks I worked at all the time. *All the time.*"

"Well, it's locked."

"So, you don't watch what they are putting in your truck when they load it?"

"They don't let me."

"Don't let you, huh?" Shelby looked at Nick, then out at the truck again. "OK, but what you're telling me is that you ain't even curious about it. Never even occurred to you to question that whole 'paper products' thing? See, that's what I find interesting"

"I just...just let it slide," said Nick, mentally searching for another topic of conversation.

"You let it slide. Yeah. I dig," said Shelby, lighting another cigarette and smiling and shrugging. "Status quo. Just go with the flow." He smiled and laughed as he looked down at the sugar packet. Some of the other patrons quickly glanced in his direction. Nick was staring out the window at the back of his truck. Through some fog a question was forming, but there was a force. Some unknown, unfelt force was pressing it flat.

Doris Day was singing "Que Sera Sera (Whatever Will Be Will Be)" in the background.

"You know what's happening in Long Beach right now, Nick?"

"The tide is rolling in." Nick shrugged. He thought it was a little funny, in a droll way, maybe.

"Yeah, you could say that. In about the last six months, just since my baby girl come along, some weird things been happening. It's like people been losing interest in life. Lots of them still go to work or school or church or whatever, but when you talk to them, I mean when I talk to them, it's like they in their own little worlds. They don't want to know about nothin'. Like they're not curious about nothin'. It's like they're just passengers on the bus or something, all just minding their own business, even when crazy things are happening right in front of them. Really hard to talk to these people. A lot of them, like my cousin Fred, are popping this new pill on the street. I think it's called 'NKD' with some numbers behind it. They call it 'knockout.' You can't go to the corner store without some punk offerin' you knockout from every alleyway now. It's disgusting."

Nick looked at Shelby. His mind went back to that guy at the Jet – Troy with greasy hair and sunglasses getting used as a mop after shouting about drugs and mind control.

"See, these people, I don't think they'd want to know what was in their trailer, either. They'd let it slide, too." He took a puff of his cigarette. "If you know what I'm sayin'."

"Well," said Nick, suddenly picking up and opening his log book. "This has been an interesting conversation."

Shelby pulled out a five-dollar bill and put it on the table. He stood up. "You take it easy out there, man," he said, shaking Nick's hand. He turned to walk away. Then, he turned back. "And remember this one message: You've got the key. Don't just let things slide."

Message. Key.
Message. Key.
Message...Key...

Nick felt something like a knotted muscle suddenly release in his back. It was like coming down off the first rise on a roller-coaster. He exhaled deeply. In an instant, all of his perceptions of his surroundings had noticeably shifted. He was disoriented. For a moment he thought it might have been the dead spot coming back, but this was different. His hands didn't tingle. He felt aware of them in a new way. He felt aware of everything in a new way. He looked at the wood-grain Formica under his placemat. He was aware of it. He was wondering about it—where it came from and how it was made. He looked up at Shelby, who smiled a little quirky grin and nodded at him as he turned. Nick felt a sheen of perspiration on his forehead. He raised a hand to his chest. He struggled to regain his breath.

Shelby slowly walked out. All eyes in the place—eyes set in white faces atop western shirts, A-line dresses, army gray-greens, gray flannel suits and ties, work coveralls, and striped sweaters from Sears—followed him as he left.

Nick's breath slowly returned. He looked back down at his manifest and his logbook. Paper products. Pomona. No load scheduled for the return.

He looked back at the trailer.

He left Shelby's five on the table and walked out, avoiding the sneer of the hostess. As he walked past the pumps outside, there was the black Mercury, almost gleaming under the harsh buzzing fluorescent lights of the canopy. No one was around it. The

Ethyl hose was stuck in the back, but no gas was flowing.

"I Only Have Eyes for You" started playing somewhere. Those first few chords. Sliding ninths.

9

Charibovi

*D*ays, nights, and perhaps even weeks and months passed.

On warmer, cloudless days the beauty of Nick's surrounding world was almost overwhelming. Nick looked forward to each day and the mood the planet would display when he opened the door of the shack. It was as if this place—the place itself— was a human person with moods and a temper. He was in the process of falling in and out of love with it, and back in love again. His enthusiasm would rise and find its apogee while he pondered the textures of the surrounding cliffs. Then a sudden cold downpour would turn the fields to mud and he'd catch himself longing for the asphalt of Chicago or even the continual *thud-dump* of expansion joints and frost heaves along Route 66. He had finally forgotten what it was like to have a coffee in one hand and a cigarette in another. He still remembered what a hot shower felt like, but even the memory of that simple pleasure was receding. He was gradually finding himself subsumed into the rhythms and textures of life in this place, as he had imagined his life would be subsumed into that of a woman should he ever find the right one. It was generally likeable, this place. But it had preferences and quirks, just like a real person. He was getting to know her better each day, and for every time that she shunned him or spat in his face, she would wrap herself around him and give him a feeling of pure belonging. He had never felt this way before anywhere else he had lived, and certainly not in the house where he grew up.

He was also getting to know Euri. At times, he felt he was getting to know her too well, too quickly. She was always with him. There was nothing about Nick's world that didn't captivate her: the truck, the army, college, how he grew up, what he did in Europe, the dark things he saw and did there, stories of people he met on the road, things he remembered from books he had read. Of course, Chicago held a special fascination for her. When she asked him about Chicago, it was as if she was preparing to hear more tales of the wonderful kingdom of Oz. Stories about the Water Tower or Wrigley Field or the amusement parks made her clasp her hands and bounce with joy.

When the conversation went quiet, Euri told him things she learned from books as well as things about her native ways. She had a wonderfully uneven education. She had memorized all the poems of Edna St. Vincent Millay but had never heard of Rudyard Kipling. She knew of Mickey Spillane and most of his characters, but had read nothing by Shakespeare. She could discuss things she had read in *No Exit* by Sartre but didn't know the national anthem. When Nick told her of something he had read, she hung on his every syllable. At times, she would relate something he said to an obscure part of an obscure novel or go on at length at how his high school friend Rob Hanson was very much like Jughead from the single *Archie* comic she owned, but also resembled Bill from the *Sun Also Rises*. Nick once asked her which character she felt she best resembled in all the books she had read. Her list of all of the interesting or appealing qualities she shared with various characters went on for some time. However, when she got to *Lolita* by Nabokov, all she would say is, "That girl is bitch." She had gotten tired of Nick correcting her pronunciation of some of the names and words, and so he let it slide for the most part. He could see no harm in letting her think Charlotte Bronte called herself "Char-*lot*-tee-ay."

Nick also learned of the ways of her people—what remained of them, and what she knew of them. She and Bacho had lived on their own, isolated since her mother had died years earlier.

They didn't keep by the Gregorian calendar at all, but Nick gathered the death had been shortly after Euri reached adolescence—likely about ten years before. Her mother had been educated at the Indian School in Phoenix, then returned to live with her tribe in an isolated canyon village near Orabi. She had been a misfit even before she left, and although she wanted to live on Hopi land, her indirect exposure to the moderate feminism and liberal thinking of the time only hardened her independent streak, making it more difficult for traditionalists to accept her. Apparently there had been a falling out between Euri's mother and her grandmother when she decided, at age twenty, to marry the much older Bacho, a wandering shepherd and hunter with a small plot in a secluded valley. The valley had been used as a sheep station by Basque herders in the past. When she left to live with him, her journey took her miles from her family of origin. It also meant the surrender of her matriarchal inheritance, as was the usual Hopi custom.

Bacho, for his part, considered himself the last of a breed. When talking of him, Euri would only say, "He's more like Apache, not Hopi," without being too definite. Euri had never been sure of where he came from, and apparently, neither had her mother. Bacho talked about the little farm as though it had been the center of a great civilization at one time, a place where many more like him had thrived. He didn't claim membership in any tribe, saying only that his people had been there for a very long time and had originally come from far away.

"What is the name of your father's people?" Nick asked one day.

"He calls them *Inde'h*. I am *Inde'h* too, but also Hopi."

"What does *Inde'h* mean?"

"It means 'people.'"

"Oh."

Apparently, Bacho had had a deep-seated ambivalence toward Hopi customs. When he'd talk of the tribe's ceremonies, it was as though he had studied them as a scholar without fully submitting himself to them. It was always *they*, not necessarily *we*. "*They* say." "*Their* ways." "*They* think." Bacho had adopted some of the Hopi ways, at least externally, in many instances. He learned rug weaving and would make his own *Katsina* outfit for ceremonies, for example. Nick gathered, however, that he did this in honor of his deceased wife and for his daughter's education more than his own observance.

Euri wore her best attempt at the traditional hair whorls of the Hopi maiden, but when Nick would admire them, she would only turn away in charmed embarrassment. Her mother had done them "the right way" only a few times before she died, and according to Euri, her current efforts, performed without the help of a female relative, were almost shameful. But, to Nick, they were adorable little buns on each side of her head, ones that sometimes moved with their own rhythm.

Nick learned the ways of the farm and the ways that predated the farm in the ancient years, learning where to go to gather firewood, water, berries, aspen bark, and other things that the wooded areas around the valley offered. He started to learn to make pottery, but after breaking down laughing as his hands touched the wet clay, he settled for just turning the wheel for Euri. He couldn't do it at the consistent speed that was required, so she found something else for him to do. He learned to herd sheep and offered to help shear them because that seemed like a good, earthy, manly thing to do. But it wasn't the season for shearing them. It was too cold. He learned how to tend goats and chickens. He tended to the horse, Mahu. Mahu was old and broken down-- an old bay gelding. Euri would hop up and ride him bareback now and then. One of Bacho's dogs took a liking to Nick and accompanied him wherever he went. Nick got strong again on a diet of lamb, eggs, tubers, corn, nuts, berries, and constant physical work.

Nick was losing the sense of what it was like to drive the truck. On occasion, he would think back on how he had lived for five years on the road. He would think back on the dissolute years spent after the army and before he drove. He would wince at the visions of absolute boredom and desperation. It had all seemed a waste to him, a million miles spent watching the world through a windshield, ignoring almost all around him. He would occasionally purse his lips and look away, holding his breath, brow furrowed. He needed to force himself to remember that it was driving that brought him here, and he never would have found this place had it not been for driving. Driving the truck was the purgatory he needed to suffer before this ascent. Still, might there have been some way for him to come upon this place more directly? For five years, any little thing could have ended his life. He could have quit. To think that a minor road accident could have prevented him from reaching this point galled him. It had all worked out in the end, but knowing it might not have reached this sweet resolution caused him to stop breathing now and again. He'd stew in his own mental funk, and then a breath would force itself into his lungs. Euri was at first concerned. But after he explained a few times, she understood. It was the symptom of bad things leaving his mind and his body. He was better now. She learned to ignore it and would sometimes just squeeze his arm or the back of his neck affectionately.

For a few hours of each afternoon, Bacho would retreat to the shack, leaving Euri and Nick to themselves. Bacho made it understood he was not to be disturbed during these times. Nick and Euri would take long walks or hang out in the lean-to that served as a barn. Nick hadn't gotten used to the smell of it yet, so their time in it was limited. Sometimes Euri would bring a book and they would take turns reading it to each other. It seemed that the one selection they could both enjoy was a Zane Gray novel. She laughed when he would read the parts spoken by the Indian character while imitating her father. One day she brought *Paradise Lost,* but Nick just cringed. He called it too heavy. She shrugged.

Nick suggested they read the Bible together, but he could tell Euri really didn't want to. He assumed it had something to do with the missionaries who were no longer welcome, and the "bad time" that they had brought. Nick didn't know many passages besides what he had heard at weddings, funerals and at Easter now and then. It just seemed like a good thing to do. He also thought it would keep his mind from wandering where he wasn't yet ready to follow.

At times, he would sit and stare at Euri, sometimes gently petting her hair or her lips. He still hadn't even kissed her. Sometimes, he'd wince when he remembered one or another of the blousy harlots he had been with while in Chicago or L.A., back when he still drove. He would remember plowing into their unresponsive bodies in some obligatory way, hearing their half-hearted words and groans of encouragement. It always distracted him. It was the sound of, "Aren't you done yet?" It was the sound of, "I need two or three others tonight to make rent." He needed to forget that. He needed to leave all that behind before he could be with Euri.

He also needed to leave behind the memories of Mary and Angela and the other one, the one whose name he couldn't quite remember. Perhaps it was "Alba," but that didn't sound quite right. All were interested in him, but unable to know him. In each of those affairs he had eventually revealed something that turned them away—something in his childhood or, perhaps, an episode of the dead spot—had alienated them. Maybe he had never allowed himself to be known, preferring to keep himself hidden in some way behind a shield. There was a certain comfort in being alone. There was a purity in his solitude.

Now, he needed to surrender that. And whenever Euri looked at him that certain way or did something to make him laugh (like bobbling her whorls of hair from side to side) or asked a question that showed she really understood him in ways that he hadn't even considered, all he wanted to do was to surrender. He wanted the old ways off of him. He wanted to be purified. And he wanted this purity only so that he could be with her, and her alone.

At night, they would all sleep in the same one-room shack. Euri's bed was nearest the door, which seemed to be the way that Bacho preferred it. Bacho slept in a bed at a right angle to Nick's, their heads almost adjacent. Nick soon adopted their habit of going to sleep soon after sunset and rising before the rooster crowed. Sometimes a dream would awaken him; a remnant of the old ways, of things that really happened. At times, it was a vivid replay of some event, similar to what he had experienced just after his arrival on the farm, back when he was still half-blind. Other times the dreams were random stories merging people and events from his life before Bacho and Euri and his life with them. The latter type was gradually replacing the former. Nick took that to be a good sign. He was happy to be dreaming again, and dreaming about his new home. He started looking forward to sleep so that the dreams would come. Sometimes he'd awaken and gaze at Euri as she slept, never leaving his bed. He'd watch her blanket fall and rise with each breath. He'd put himself into a trance, imagining that he couldn't move his legs again. Then, he'd fall back asleep and into another dream.

Nick and Euri were washing clothes together near the well.

"I want to go to Chicago," said Euri. She abruptly got to her feet. Nick looked up at her. He noticed it was still cold on the mountain. The sunlight itself seemed cold.

"Why?" he asked. He really didn't need to.

"You tell so many stories about it. About the river. About Russian Division. About the trains. About the grass museum. There are so many more books there."

Grass museum. Nick pondered.

"Oh, the *Field* Museum!" he said with a laugh. "Yes, it's pretty special, I guess."

"Let's go." She had already showed a streak of the resolute that ran through her. It would occasionally surface, letting Nick know that the shyness, the humility, and the avoidance was all were part of an act she had acquired somehow.

"We'd need to leave this behind," said Nick, his hands cold in the rinsing water. "What would your dad do?" Nick really didn't want to leave the farm.

"He raised me on his own. He can live on his own. He's strong. He's an Indian."

"He's an old man now. He was younger when he raised you." Nick was regretting making Chicago sound so glamorous. He wasn't sure what he'd find if he ever returned there-- what the company would say. He didn't know if his apartment on Diversey was still in his name. He didn't know if he had been gone a week or a month or even a year. He didn't know what he'd do for a living, or even if he'd want to do anything. On one level, he thought of Chicago as a miraculous place of legend, having seen it through Euri's fantasies. But the rational part of him knew it to be a shithole of deceit, disappointment, and death.

In the back of his mind, there was the fear that the two men in the black Mercury were out there still. Maybe they had given up after seeing the truck explode. Maybe they had written him off. If he suddenly reappeared, what would happen?

"Nick, we are young. We need to go before we are old too."

"You're younger than me."

Euri gave him *the look*. He started to wither. She was silent for a while, then turned back to the washing. There was tension. She didn't like being reminded of her age, especially in any way that grew barriers between them.

"Look, Euri," he began while wringing out a blanket. "I told you about Chicago because it's my hometown. It's where I grew up. It's a big city. It's kinda ugly. It's also where my mom drank herself to death, and my dad killed himself in a garage. I stayed there because it was home, in a way. But now I feel this is my home. I've made this my home with you and Bacho and the dogs and the—"

"You're a coward. Like *Charibovi*." she shot back. Her eyes darted at him. Her lips were curled in a half sneer.

That came suddenly, and it stung. If it hadn't nearly made Nick laugh, he might have been enraged. An Indian maiden in native garb making a sophisticated reference to a fleeting nickname given to a character in one of Flaubert's novels.

"Charibovi, eh? You think I'm like that?" he was piqued and bemused at the same time.

"Yes. You know the world. You have been in the world. You have been to England and France and Germany and Chicago. But you were treated mean there, so you come here and think it's nice. You run away." She glared at him and corrected herself, intensely. "You *ran* away. And now you want me to hide you. You think you got Emma. I am not Emma, but you are Charibovi!"

"I *didn't*..." Nick felt something rising up inside of him, and it wasn't affectionate. "I was brought here. You forget that. I was brought here. Your father brought me here. I spent days, *days* telling you both I needed to leave."

"He is not making you stay," she said, simply, while wringing out a pair of her father's jeans. For a young girl who had been raised by an old Indian guy among various sheep and chickens, she had a lot of verve.

Nick was feeling a wild combination of emotions. He was angry at her, he was doubting himself, he was wondering where he had lost the plot, or if there had been a plot to lose in the first place, and yet, when he looked at her back and her hips flex as she bent down to wring out a shirt, he could have taken her right then and savored every ounce and whiff and pore of her.

"I don't want to take you away from your father. He loves you." Nick gently placed his hand on her shoulder. Euri's hands went limp in the bucket where the shirts soaked. She slumped.

"Nick." She sighed, an air of emotional exhaustion overtaking her. "Your father loved you, too. He stood in your way. You let him for a while. But then you didn't let him. You moved on. You left. And you knew what was—"

Nick raged. He grabbed her shoulders and jerked her around to face him. He yanked her to him and shook her. She gasped and turned her head away from his face, trying to draw back away from him. "Look, *look you...*" He was gritting his teeth. At first he spoke softly, angrily through his teeth, but it built to a crescendo that was almost a shout. Euri kept her face away. "I chose to stay when I was sixteen. It was my choice. When I was eighteen, I had to go. If I didn't go, I would have been drafted. I told you that. I did *not* know! I did *not* know what he was going to do when I came back. I did *not* know he was that unstable. I did *not* know I would come back expecting..."

Euri turned to look at him. Her gaze was cold and defiant. "And if you had? What then, *Nick Pente?*" She almost snarled his name. "What then?" Her voice was again quiet, slow, and determined. She stared into him. Her whorls were perfectly still.

He looked into her brown and saffron eyes. He could see every grain in each iris. He felt tightness in his chest. He looked at the hair bound up in the whorls on each side of her head. He released his grip. Then, with his hands suddenly empty, he felt an overwhelming emptiness. He wrapped his arms around her and slid down her knees. He was in tears, his chest heaving to carry the weight of his breath. She ran her hands through his hair and then joined him on the ground. They said nothing. The tears flowed.

As they lay there together, Nick looked up in the cold, cloudless sky. Something occurred to him, a remnant of a reading assignment barely remembered from college years before -- one he probably hadn't completed.

"You know," he said, "This story, our story -- you know what it reminds me of?"

"What?" Nick's head was resting on her lap. She stroked his hair.

"*Paradise Lost*. Here we are in this Eden. We don't need to do anything but be ourselves and work to feed ourselves. Most of the time, it doesn't even seem like work, when I'm with you, at least. We've got your dad here, and things are nice. But now you come up with this, and it's like you've been talking to the snake."

Euri's hand stopped in mid-stroke. She frowned, then started stroking his hair again, this time more slowly. Nick stared off at the mountains in the distance. A hawk soared over one of the peaks, moving in circles over something below.

"Nick, I think you are the snake, and Adam and Eve, they were in bubble." She paused and moved her fingers through his hair more resolutely, in silence. "They made a decision. It was time to go."

Over the peak, Nick saw the hawk fold its wings and dive for its prey.

10

Don't Look Back

Through some means of mental preparation, Nick awoke the next morning while Bacho and Euri still slept. It was dark but for the nearly full moon.

In the evening before, he had wandered around the ranch, avoiding the campfire. He had taken an early meal and said nothing. Euri and Bacho said nothing to him. He needed to think, and the both seemed to know it. His gaze kept moving toward the mountain in the west of the valley. After dinner he wished Euri a good night, then quietly snuck into the shack and lay down. He had slept in his clothes.

In the morning, he silently slipped into his shoes, being careful to not make the bed or floorboards creak. He had found the nailheads that indicated where the floor joists were. Carefully, he walked on them to keep his steps quiet. By putting upward pressure on the squeaking door's hinges, he was able to leave quietly. He ran to the barn and slipped into the thick wool poncho and hat he had left there. As he left the barn, one of Bacho's dogs—the one Bacho called by only a few clicks of his tongue and otherwise seemed nameless—awakened and followed him.

Nick walked down the trail towards the west wall of the valley. The first traces of rosy-fingered dawn were coming up over the eastern mountains, which were slightly lower than those in the West. Nick walked along a path that seemed to head to the center portion of the peaks. It had been warm a few days previous, so any traces of the snow from the week before, or however long it had been, were gone. The wind was still. The cold air filled his lungs.

The trail ended about a quarter of the way up the mountain at a rock outcropping that resembled a cliff. After Nick surveyed it for a few seconds, it seemed like something that should be climbed. He placed his non-marking, oil-resistant nonskid black leather shoe in a gap that seemed almost like a step. Halfway up, it occurred to him that he might need to descend it as well at some time, but he figured he'd find a way when that time came—if it came.

Bacho's dog sat and whined. After Nick was a few feet above the ground, the dog took off back down the trail.

Winded, Nick crested the top of the rock and saw that the trail resumed almost exactly above where it had ended at the base of the climb. It led him back into a wooded area.

Finally, he felt enough distance and time to replay the events from the day before. He thought of how Euri had changed from a smart, joyous, curious if somewhat frivolous girl one moment to a resolute manipulator the next. But the more he thought about it, the more he seemed to love her, in fact. His love had become reinforced with something akin to the real key to a man's heart: respect.

He thought back on a conversation he had overheard between a preacher and a young beatnik at another truck stop in Missouri. The young man had been going on about how if there was a God, He should be treated with respect and not fear. The old preacher pulled back and said, "Son, respect and fear is the *same damned thing*."

So, maybe that's what it was. He now, for the first time, feared Euri. He feared her in the way that could be called "respect," which didn't mean that he thought she would do him physical harm or lead him to doom if he didn't give into her demands. No, it was a different sort of fear. He feared that he was no longer with an adorable, charming girl. He feared he had found a beautiful, intelligent, strong woman who could and would demand more from him than he had ever been able to give. Their relationship had entirely changed over the course of about two minutes spent wringing out blankets by the well.

He wasn't sure what to think of this new thing—this new sensation. The girls he had known before never demanded much of him. But then, Nick had never really given them the opportunity. He met Mary when she was doing candy-stripe work at the VA in Chicago shortly after he came back from the war. She was pretty and kind, and after knowing her a few weeks, he started to think he might have found the girl he could marry. But when he'd have a moment of introspection, she wasn't able to cope at all. She needed to be constantly reassured and stimulated in some childish way. She reminded Nick of his mother in certain ways. When Nick had a blackout one night during a date and he couldn't remember where he parked his car on State Street, she nearly went into a panic. They didn't talk after that.

Angela was much more tolerant of Nick's tune-outs, being a somewhat introverted college-office typist herself. But one night, while out drinking, Nick walked past her to flirt with her friend. He honestly didn't see Angela. She had faded into the crowd.

And Alba—or whatever her name was—well, she was just a freak.

But then there were bar girls and party girls and whatever one would call girls who knocked on his hotel door in the middle of the night wearing cocktail dresses or short skirts and stockings. There were even a few lone women who made a show of deliberately sitting down beside him at the counters of rural truck stops and flashing their false eyelashes, all done up as they were in cotton dresses from Woolworth's. All his memories of these girls seemed to coalesce into a glob of something left on a top sheet that was then tossed in the corner for the maid to handle in the morning.

Somewhere in him was the notion that all of his prior deeds could be forgiven and left behind. There was the spark of a desire flashing now. Something told him he wanted it all washed off of him. He wanted to be the man that Euri's interest suggested he could be: a man worthy of a woman like her.

And the more he thought about it, the more he feared he could never, ever be that man. His heart alternately rose and sank as he walked along.

The path was hard to follow. It led Nick to another rock outcropping that invited him to climb up and over. The sun was nearly up by now. He wondered what the others would think when they awoke. Maybe they would assume he had fled back to his old ways. Maybe Bacho would believe it was the TV or the noise or the pace and excitement of the modern world that lured him. Euri would suspect that he just wasn't the man for her after all, and that he had lost his nerve at the first sign that she wasn't to be used or patronized. Maybe she was a little girl after all, and her heart would be broken, or maybe she'd call upon that inner well of annealed iron he had witnessed emerging in her. Maybe she'd just resolve to move on with her life.

But then, he had a fascinating thought. Even though he had walked perhaps two miles by then -- farther than he had ever been from the farm since he had been dragged there – he still felt something pulling him back.

Standing on the top of the rocky ledge, he turned to the east and saw the sun starting to illuminate the mountaintops on the opposite side of the valley. He couldn't see the valley from where he stood. The peaks looked different from this vantage point. They seemed even more massive, wider than when viewed from the farm. He turned to look around him. Above the trees, in the distance was the hint of the rolling plains near Seligman. It was somewhere beyond the mountains, a couple thousand feet below, a few more miles away. He tried to think of what might be going on down there in that little town. Was there still a search party? Had there been a memorial service? Had there been any casualties on the train when it crashed into the truck? If he could go back there, would he be greeted or detained? Would he be thrown into jail? Captured by the two men in the Mercury? Would he be greatly relieved at the sparse comforts the little town offered, even if he were tossed into jail? He caught himself thinking of it as an entirely different world--and a somewhat threatening one at that. It was just as he once looked at those abandoned-seeming shacks on lonely plains in the distance as he drove by. He was on the other side of the looking glass.

That reminded him: Euri hadn't read *Alice in Wonderland*. He'd have to find her a copy. Somehow. Sometime.

He felt the farm pulling him back.

The sun had now risen and was illuminating the rocks on which he stood. He looked to see if the trail resumed on another side. As he turned, something caught his eye. One part of the rock out-cropping was more vertical, forming a secondary ledge about four feet tall at one side. It ran about twenty feet along the edge, forming something that resembled a granite wall. There were some rocks stacked in ways that looked deliberate. Slowly, he approached.

Leaned up against the wall were a series of sandstone tablets, most perhaps eighteen inches tall. One or more figures were etched on each tab-let. Some were accented with dyes and colors, others were just line drawings. Some colors had faded in the sun. Some had obviously been re-etched and repainted dozens or perhaps hundreds of times. At that point in the sun's arc, only their topmost edges were illuminated. Nick saw male and female fig-ures, some arranged as families, some infants, some children by themselves. Nick wondered if this was a tomb of some sort, but the rocky surface seemed to suggest otherwise. Set on the tops of some of the figure drawings were feathers and branches or pieces of elk horn. A small section of sheepskin dec-orated one of them. He found that one fascinating.

This was a place of worship. He had heard Bacho talk of his fathers and their fathers. It seemed that he had stumbled upon a temple to the clan's ancestors, which had probably been visited for hundreds if not thousands of years.

He began to think of his father, then his mother. Always in that order. That was probably because he felt he had barely known his mother. She had been absent or distracted for so much of his early life that it almost seemed she had a walk-on part in the movie of his life so far. When the family participated in social events (and it wasn't often), she would sometimes come along --sometimes. Usually, she was silent when out and about with others. If something happened to upset her, neither Nick nor his father would find out about it until the door of the car shut on the way home. Then, the dam would break. Every imagined slight, every faux pas, every sidelong glance was noted and remembered and recited again and again in a long-running diatribe that lasted the entire way home, reaching a crescendo of sobbing, shrieking, and hand-wringing just as they turned down their street, with his father trying but consistently failing to reassure her that the women at the theater or the department store or the war-bond rally were not blaming her for her four miscarriages and that the priest didn't think she was a whore for wearing a skirt that didn't touch her shoes. When they would get home, she would make a stop in the kitchen to anxiously grab a bottle of gin or vodka or whatever was handy, then sequester herself in her bedroom upstairs with a slam of the door. His father would calmly put on his slippers and start to read the paper or do a crossword at the kitchen table, occasionally cleaning his glasses as his wife's shrieks and screams echoed from somewhere up the staircase. Nick would sit in the living room and either color, listen to the radio, read, or play guitar, depending on which phase of his life that particular evening fell. Eventually, the shrieking would die down to a sobbing murmur, and Nick's dad would shout out from behind the newspaper he was reading in the kitchen.

"Nicky! Cubs won yesterday. Bryant threw a one-hitter. Attaboy! Attaboy!"

"Nicky! City Hall's finally going to pave that alley. About time! About time!"

"Nicky! The new Packards are out. Looking snazzy! Looking snazzy!"

"Nicky! They found that schmuck who robbed the abbey. The bastard! The bastard!"

"Nicky! I need a five-letter tree. Starts with 'M.' Starts with 'M.'"

Those were Nick's memories of his ancestors. When he'd ask, there were some stories about a great grandfather Constantin on his father's side. He had died before Nick was born, but seemed to have been a celebrity in the family. "A brilliant man! Came to this country with a nickel, and it wasn't even an American nickel. Then, next thing you know, he's got a nut stand, and then two, and then three. By about the age of forty, he was the nut king of La Grange!" Unfortunately, an accident had claimed his life shortly after Nick's dad's birth. The nature of the accident had been judged too harsh or provocative for young ears.

His mother didn't talk about her relatives, and it was assumed that they didn't talk about her, either.

The warmest memory he had of his mother was of her comforting him that one time. It was when he had suffered an episode at summer camp at age twelve. That might have been the first time, actually. The camp organizers had called his parents. They immediately drove all the way to Winnetka to get him. Nick had more or less recovered when the car pulled into camp. Nick remembered being flabbergasted to see his mother in the passenger seat. Usually, it was only his father who attended anything he did. He'd look out from the basketball court and see his father's balding head and glasses. Same thing at graduation, at his piano recital, when he was sitting on Santa's lap, and just about any other time. He never expected to see his mom. Nick rode in the backseat with her on the way back home to Chicago that time, his head cradled between her breasts while she spoke soothingly to him and stroked his head. The mood was somber. He actually remembered his dad was the one who was upset that time.

Nick was in a stone-age chapel dedicated to ancestors that lived in even more primitive ways than did Euri and Bacho, and yet they likely knew more about where they came from than Nick did, even with the benefits of sophisticated record-keeping, the telephone, photography, mail service, and all the tools of modern scientific culture. Nick wondered why.

The best answer: They had decided it actually mattered to them. They were aware of the importance of awareness. And they couldn't think of much that was more important than the awareness of their own origins.

He crouched down beside the altar. There was one etching that looked more current than the rest. It had a small piece of sheepskin sheltering and cushioning it. It was a depiction of a young woman. This etching seemed subtler than the others—of finer line. The woman was holding a pose with her chin up. She faced the viewer in a three-quarter view. He eyes were strong and defiant. Given the medium, the detailing was remarkable. Nick stared into the eyes.

"She was wife. She dead now," Nick jolted upright and turned.

"Bacho!"

"We thought you go back to town. Run away."

"How did you know I was here?"

"Dog come back. Woof, woof, woof. He run off. I follow him."

"So, the dog told you?" Nick grinned.

"Yeah. Told on you. Hehehe." Bacho smiled. He strode around in front of the etchings. He looked off in the distance, then crouched down to look at the stone edge more closely. It was as if he were speaking to the stones themselves. He grunted softly as his hand moved over the rough granite. He looked up at Nick.

"So," said Bacho. "You better now. You going to leave?"

This caught Nick off guard. He didn't know if Bacho was telling him he must leave, or just asking him his intentions.

"I don't want to leave. I'd rather stay."

"You gotta think about that."

"Am I welcome here. . . still?"

"Yeah, you welcome to stay." Bacho looked down the row of etchings. He breathed deeply. His saffron-brown eyes slowly lifted to take in the mountain summit, still above them by a few hundred feet. Bacho rose to his feet. "But you gotta think about that. You made of stars, too. Some stars move different."

Nick stood awkwardly while Bacho looked at his feet and then at the row of etchings. Nick moved to the side. He didn't want to be in the way. After a few seconds, Bacho assumed a stance with his legs apart, standing squarely in front of the altar. He slowly raised his hands above him, reaching for the sky, then closed his eyes, and bent his head down. He said a few native words under his breath. Nick didn't know what to do, so he gathered one hand in another and held them before him, his feet slightly apart in an at-ease pose. His face took on the somber expression he reserved for funerals or memorial services. After a minute or so, Bacho broke off his worship—if that's what it was—and looked back toward the interloper.

Nick tried to discern where he stood with Bacho. Was he offended that Nick had sneaked out and violated this space? Feeling very tentative, he didn't look at the old man directly. Instead, he fixed his eyes back on the etching he had been admiring.

"How long ago?" ventured Nick.

"Long time. Euri only baby then."

"What was her name?"

"She call *Hehewuti*. Mean 'warrior spirit.' Her mothers are Hopi."

Nick half-smiled. "I see."

Bacho looked in his eyes. "You see, eh? You think you know her daughter now. My daughter. Little girl. Euri." He smiled.

"Another warrior spirit."

"Yes, you learn. Hehehe."

"Did she tell you about—"

"No, but I see. Other ways to see."

"So, what do you think? What do you think about what you see?"

"Why is that important?"

"Well, Euri is your daughter."

"Euri is made of stars. Just like you, me. I tell her do right thing. Sometimes, she do other things. Some stars move different."

Nick was at a loss. He didn't know what this meant for him and Euri.

"Do you approve?"

Bacho looked at him. He looked at him for a long time. His expression was blank. His eyes barely moved.

"OK, I tell you what you do. You stay here all day. When sun start to go down, you come back. Later today, you see. After you see, come back. If you don't see..."

At that, Bacho nodded, then smiled almost imperceptibly. He turned and slowly walked back down the trail Nick had followed. Then he stopped, just before he left the edge of the rock. He looked back at Nick and nodded once more.

And then he turned and walked off.

So Nick sat, and he stood, and sat, and stood for hours, staring at the etchings of the ancestors. It was like being at the Art Institute of Chicago, where he would sit and stare at paintings for hours, allowing their shapes and colors to make their impression on his psyche. He found a shard of sandstone off to the side of the escarpment, no bigger than his hip pocket. He picked it up and looked at it for a while. Then, he looked at the etchings leaned against the wall. Something in him didn't want to follow what came to mind. He wasn't an artist. The extent of his artistry was limited to playing some interesting chords on guitar now and then. He looked at the etching of Euri's mother again. There was such talent expressed in each stroke. Someone did the etching out of love. Every little miniscule stroke, probably done over the course of years—was carved with just enough relief to bring out the curves of the distinctly Indian nose that he recognized in Euri. He wondered how long Hehewuti must have sat for Bacho to get that look. He knew it likely couldn't have been done from a photograph. And yet here it was, a carving that shone forth with life because of the life that had been put into it by the loving hands of the artist. He reached down and picked up a sharp piece of granite, just large enough to fit in his fingers. He held it and stared at the grain. How long had it sat there until he had come along?

He heard a crunching sound a ways off, unmistakably footsteps. Bacho, back again? Maybe Euri? Off in the distance through the trees, he could hear the footsteps getting closer. He stood.

In a moment, there appeared a tan cowboy duster, topped off with a worn straw hat. Somewhere in between was the worn face of age: a grizzled old man. He emerged from the trees, not really looking anywhere in particular but slowly and confidently walking in Nick's direction. He arrived near the edge of the escarpment. He looked around. He was thin and slightly hunchbacked. He wore work boots that were covered in a layer of dust. His face was stoic and covered with lines. It was as though a part of the desert had taken human form.

Nick was in the state of mind that told him that anything that happened was to be accepted. He was letting things be. He smiled.

"Name's Hannigan," the man finally said, flatly. His voice had a low, dry rumble.

"Nick Pente."

They stood in silence for a while, each looking around at the etchings and the surrounding trees. Hannigan finally crouched down to one of the etchings. Nick became defensive for the first time. He had heard of grave robbers and vandals.

"Most of these are Hopi or some other Pueblo tribe," Hannigan finally began. "You got your Katsinas and your crows and hawks. But ol' Bacho, he's not one of them." He pointed over at the etching of Hehewuti. "Man's got different sensibilities."

"You know Bacho?" Nick asked, slightly taken aback.

"Yes, I know Bacho." Hannigan walked over to the etching of Bacho's dead wife -- Euri's mother. "He's a kind and gentle soul. I've known him for ages, it seems."

Hannigan didn't seem like he was there to bag artifacts for resale, nor to senselessly destroy this place. He knelt on one knee next to Hehewuti's portrait.

"She was so beautiful," he said. He brought his hand to his chin thoughtfully.

"You knew her? Euri's mother?"

"Yes, you could say so." He turned to Nick. A glint came into his eye, and then a smile. "As much as a man can know a tornado or a blizzard or an avalanche or a mountain." He guffawed, almost silently.

"Bacho saved my life," said Nick.

"Yes, he does that sorta thing. Did it for me, too." Hannigan was smoothing the dirt in front of the portrait.

"You from Seligman?"

"No, here."

"All your life?"

"Since Bacho found me, that is. Yes." Nick was silent. Hannigan must have felt he owed him some further explanation, though he wasn't the kind to volunteer much. "Used to live at a hay camp down near Paulden. Went out wandering one day on my horse. Didn't know where I was goin'. Just didn't want to be there anymore."

There was more silence as Hannigan straightened the sheepskin at the top of the portrait.

"I got up past the trail down there by Seligman. Went a few more miles, and my horse threw a shoe. He got tripped up goin' down a little gorge, and he fell on me. Thought I was set to die. Musta laid there for a day or two. Horse broke his neck." Hannigan stood up and winced, squeezing the back of his neck. "Sad thing. He was a damn good horse."

Hannigan walked over to one of the boulders and slowly sat down.

"So, I wake up, and there's old Bacho. And I'm in bed, but I can't move. Don't know how he did it, but some of that old Indian medicine must work." He stared at the portrait of Hehewuti.

"So, how long have you been here? On this mountain?"

"Brother, I lost count of the days. Seems like forever, but then again, seems like an afternoon."

Hannigan was as outside of time as the Indians. Nick looked at him more closely. His worn and sun-faded duster could have been from the 1880s, though the ranchers in northern Arizona still dressed that way in modern times, and they still rode horses. A question occurred to Nick as he gazed at this man, who was both more familiar and yet more strange to him for being from the culture down the hill, the one Nick hadn't seen in what seemed like forever.

"Do you ever want to go back? Back down the hill?" Nick asked.

Hannigan nodded and smiled. "There ain't too much left down there for me anymore, son."

Nick smiled too. He knew the feeling. "There's not much I want down that hill. Not much I really want at all." It was good to feel he had the validation of someone else from his culture.

"Your situation's different. You can't stop wantin' yet." Hannigan winced, then looked off in the distance toward Seligman. "I know you think you can. But that just ain't so. You still got some diggin' to do to set things right. You gotta keep wanting for now."

Nick's brow furrowed.

Hannigan turned to face Nick, then got to his feet. "I dunno where you came from, mister. But, I can tell you that you can thank your lucky stars the day you met Bacho and his girl. And..." Hannigan paused, stretched his back, and looked at the sun rising over the mountains. "I can tell you that if you ever wanna leave, there's just one thing you gotta remember." He turned his head away from the altar and spat. "You don't look back."

At that, Hannigan tipped his hat and turned, slowly walking off toward the west.

Nick turned back to the altar, then took a seat.

Sometime in the afternoon, with the sun moving fast toward the western sky, it occurred to Nick what Bacho meant. He wasn't sure if something inside of him had finally left, or if something new had entered.

He had started to hear things. The wind would move through the gorges and valleys in the mountain and through the trees, and if he listened carefully, it seemed to have the cadence and tone of speech. As the afternoon sun warmed the mountain, the sounds changed. They almost seemed to get chatty. The setting sun made them sound like giggles and sighs.

The sun was disappearing behind the mountain where the temple lay when Nick saw the farm again. It had a compact beauty when viewed from on high at this hour. The sheep had gathered near the warm side of the pen. The fire had been stoked. The barn and the shack appeared to have been arranged by the very hand of God. It was heartbreaking in its beauty.

Nick saw Euri standing near the fire. Bacho was sitting on a stump. She looked in Nick's direction as he approached. She crossed her arms. As he got near, the dog ran to meet him, jumping about in a merry caper. Nick wasn't sure what Euri's face would say. As he got closer, he saw her expression was flat. Then, a hint of a smile appeared. She turned back to the fire and ladled him a bowl of stew. Bacho only looked at Nick and nodded. Once.

When Bacho had gone off to bed, Nick reached into his pocket and pulled out the shard of sandstone. He had carved into it a single musical note—a quarter note. It lacked the staff behind it for reference, but he liked to think it was the high note he couldn't hit before. He gave it to Euri. She smiled more brightly than the sun had shone that day. She stared into his eyes and clasped his hands. He looked into hers, and it was as though some far-off voice had told him a secret about her, and about them together.

11

Singers and a Little Mouse

The next day proceeded uneventfully, and Nick's little excursion wasn't mentioned at all. T he night began like most of the others. T hey were gathered around the fire. Euri had slaughtered a chicken earlier in the day, and it made a good dinner cooked in a stew with hominy. Euri and Nick sat closer together this night than they had before. Bacho seemed to notice it.

"You kids, you do washing, eh?" he asked between bites.

"Yes," said Nick. "Lots and lots of it." He smiled.

"That good. Clean clothes." There was an awkward tone in Bacho's speech. The grunts were missing. He seemed strangely tentative.

Nick cleared his throat. He looked at Euri for a moment, then back at Bacho. "You know, Bacho, where I come from, we have machines that do washing. You know that? Don't need to use hands anymore. Get a lot more done that way." Euri smiled and got up to stoke the fire with a stick.

"Hey-yeah," said Bacho. "Machines. They catch fire. Blow up."

"Well, no." Nick laughed. "Washing machines usually don't do that. Unlike trucks and trains. And even trucks and trains don't usually do that."

"Yours did."

"Yeah, well, that was a special circumstance. Most of the time, machines don't blow up. They really help people. People have a lot more time to do things like read and teach their kids and play music and things— all thanks to machines. That's what it's like in Chicago, where I come from. No one there spends a whole day on washing. Some even have these dryers. They don't need to hang up their laundry in the sun or by the fire or anything. The clothes come out all dry and warm in about an hour or so. Just like that." Nick was trying to sound positive and cheerful.

Bacho grunted. He took another bite.

Nick felt he was on a roll. Even if he wasn't, there was no turning back now.

"We have TV. Have you ever seen TV? It's like this picture box. Moving picture box you keep in your house. It's like a movie, and I know you know what a movie is because you were telling me about that Western you saw back when you were a kid down in Seligman. That one with Tom Mix."

"I saw one movie." And with that, Bacho let on that it was probably enough.

"Yes, well, TV is like that but you have three or four channels, and you can see movies all day for free, if you like. They have shows with entertainers. Ed Sullivan; you'd like him. Jugglers and singers and a little mouse."

"I have sheep."

"I know, but what I am telling you is that there's a big world out there full of new things, and I think Euri deserves to see more of it than what she sees here. She reads everything you bring her, and she loves it. She loves you! But she's young, and she wants to see the world."

Bacho set down his bowl to the side. The moon was almost full and was about a third of the way across the sky. He looked up at the moon and raised his hands above his head. Nick looked at Euri. She looked back, but offered no response. Bacho started to hum to himself. After a few seconds, he stopped and turned his eyes to the starry horizon above the mountains to the west and slowly got to his feet. He cleared his throat.

"I have seen a lot," he began. "I am old Indian guy, but I have seen some with my eyes. I have seen some in other ways, without eyes. I have heard stories from my father, and his father, and many fathers before. They knew of your ways. White ways." Bacho paced slowly in tight circles near the fire.

"The big road, the one where you crash your truck: Six-six. That not new. Many years ago, our people walk that road. Many fathers. We once were many, we people. We ran from *Thavgyalyal* to *Thilgsvgov* and even to *Wiii Baggwa* and even farther to trade with the *Dineh*. We had great cities. We had many people. Then, the white man come and bring death. Our people died, one after other. Some lived, very few. Euri and I are last—last of my people here. I am not Hopi. We are not Navajo. We are different, but all are gone. Except for us."

Euri cleared her throat and said a few words in her native language, tentatively, looking more at Bacho than Nick.

"And Euri, she like Hopi because her mother Hopi. But I am not Hopi. And she my daughter."

Euri pursed her lips and turned away.

Bacho continued. "When you talk about your world, your people and land, it about always death. You go to German and kill. You come back, and your father and mother, dead. I see you crash your truck, and you almost dead. People on train—dead? I don't know. The men chasing you, the ones who looked bad. They wanted death. You talk about Chicago and boat sinking and fires and disease and Al Capone, and there is more death. All you talk about is death, because that's all the white man knows: kill and win. But that, is losing."

With that, there was silence. The cold wind made the trees rustle in the distance. Euri pulled the poncho around her more tightly. Nick touched her shoulder.

Nick cleared his throat, and it slowly began. "Bacho, no. It's not all death. There's life there. Great, beautiful life. We've come so far beyond where we were. We can cure diseases now. We can prevent diseases. Little kids who would have died only a few years ago are living now. Old people are living longer—longer and happier lives. We're discovering new things all the time that make people live longer, and even let women have kids when they thought they were sterile."

Bacho looked at him and smirked, then shook his head. "Euri," he asked. "How many die in big war, where Nick was soldier?"

Euri looked up from her chair. "About fifty million people, the book said."

Bacho looked at Nick. "In my land, with my people, we don't have word for 'million.' Euri, she tell me is more than all the stars at night, but fifty of that. All dead. Children."

"Yes, it was a horrible war. I fought in it. I had friends die. I was hurt in it. But, it's over, and—"

"Now you have a big bomb. You have a bomb to kill the whole world. Everybody." Bacho waved his hand in a sweeping gesture.

"It's not going to be used. In fact, it's good that we have it because it keeps others—"

"At night, sometimes the sky light up over there." He pointed to the west "They use the big bomb. The missionaries, the Christian men, they told me. They told us to leave, to not breathe. They say was bad for sheep."

"Yes, it's a test. They were only testing."

"It's all death. All of it. White man don't just hate Indian. We gone now, most of us. So, they hate and kill each other. White man bomb and kills each other now."

"Bacho, look, I know what you say is true, in a way. We have killed and killed and then killed some more. But, I want you to know this." Nick got to his feet and walked to Bacho's side. Something had come to mind--something he had read about only a few weeks before the crash. It was still the talk of most conversations at truck stops and bars. He pointed to the night sky. "Up there right now, up in the sky, there's a star we put there. The Russians put a star up there, made by man. By white men. Right now, it's circling the earth. It's been up there a few months already."

Bacho looked to the sky to try to see this new star that Nick was talking about. He grunted and turned his gaze back to the ground. "You and I, we made of stars already. Everything is made of stars. So, white man put something back up there. That star move different. Not too important."

Euri seemed to cringe.

Nick continued, undeterred. "But see, that's only the first step. They're talking about putting a man on the moon in just a few years. Yes! Imagine that! Men on the moon. From that point, men will go to the stars a few years after, and the only way we are going to do that—and I know this because it's true—is if we..." Nick paused to take a deep breath. "If we stop the wars and never, ever fight like we did again. We can't destroy each other while trying to move out to other stars. The only way it is going to happen is if we get over this and stop the killing. So it's done. It's over. So, Bacho, this is the point. Now, you can say that I'm only death, and that's all I come from. But Euri is younger than I am, and she will see more than you and I will. I think she will see a world that's entirely different than the one I know and that you've heard of. She might even go to the stars, herself. But the only way she will see that is if..." Bacho looked at him. "You let me take her back with me."

Bacho was silent. He stared at Nick for a moment, then started pacing again. It was getting cold. Euri stoked the fire. Nick sat down next to her.

"Father," she said softly but with that same streak of the resolute Nick had come to know. "I want to go to Chicago...with Nick."

Bacho turned his back to them. They heard him sniff. He grunted. Then, he straightened his posture. He started walking. Nick and Euri watched him disappear. The darkness engulfed him as he headed toward the mountainside.

Somewhere in the distance, a coyote howled.

"Where is he going?" asked Nick.

"He's going to talk to his ancestors. Our ancestors."

Nick noticed that Euri had already started to distance herself from him, perhaps subconsciously. They stood in silence. It was an uncomfortable few seconds.

"I think I said what I needed to say." Nick was hoping for some sort of affirmation.

"You said what I think." Euri was stoic and sparse.

"When will he be back?"

"In the morning, maybe."

Nick held Euri close to him. He felt her body relaxing against his, her gentle curves conforming to him with a feeling of surrender. In her hair he inhaled the aroma of juniper wood and sage. He looked down into her in the eyes, and then after gathering and clasping her hands together, he turned toward the shack. He was exhausted. Some specific images ran across his mind. He tried to ignore them.

As he lay down in bed covering himself with blankets, the door opened. It was Euri. They smiled at each other. He watched her get into her bed, snuggle under the blankets, then blow out the single candle that lit the room.

"Goodnight, Euri."

"Goodnight, Nick."

Sleep came quickly. Nick had put himself into that state of mind where he didn't dwell on things. He was letting it slide.

Soon after he drifted off he looked up from the vibrating white "T" that gradually overcame his vision and realized he was back inside his truck again, downshifting the transmission to slow the load on a long descent out of Flagstaff, through Ash Fork, and into Seligman. It was very early on that Thursday morning – the last Thursday morning he could remember -- and he was still shaking off the few minutes of fitful sleep he had grabbed in a parking lot in Flagstaff. The afternoon and evening before, he had driven all the way from Acoma while staring in his mirrors. And then at the Heartland he had felt his life begin to change. The shocking conversation with Shelby still rang in his ears. He was ambivalent. He didn't want it, whatever this feeling it was. Storm clouds occasionally obscured the moon. The mirrors reflected only a single, distant pair of headlights behind him. They would disappear when the road behind him dipped or he accelerated, only catch up to him briefly when he slowed down. It was like his mental state was teasing itself. He was in between, somehow.

He couldn't get Shelby's question out of his mind. It had never occurred to him to question the manifest. Why had it never occurred to him? No matter how he tried to justify it to himself, he couldn't dismiss that one question. It suddenly seemed incredibly strange to him—not that he was being paid to drive a load of some sort of dreary consumer product across most of the country and then return with an empty trailer in a truck that got only three miles per gallon of hi-test. No, that wasn't the question. It didn't even seem strange to him that he was paid more money than he could typically spend in the minimal free time the job afforded. The question kept coming back. Why had he just gone along with the routine without even being tempted to question it? Why did it seem like the trailer behind him didn't even exist?

Why?

The question nagged at him now as it never had before. For five years, he had successfully ignored it. It was nothing. Now, it was jabbing at him like a stone in his shoe. He tried to force it down. It didn't work. It came right back. It jabbed and jabbed at him. He felt his war wound pounding at his shoulder. He hadn't felt it in years. He noticed himself breathing heavily. He looked down at the dashboard. He noticed the green glow of the lights in a way he hadn't before. The vibration of the engine and the road were coming through to him in new ways. And there, in the middle of the steering wheel, was the mystical, almost-glowing T. Its essential strangeness grasped out at him, seemingly for the first time ever.

He looked in his mirrors. He double-clutched down and let the horses run. The gauges swung around, the turbocharger kicked in and suddenly his back was pressed into the seat. The speedometer climbed. No one would be on the road at this hour. Seventy, seventy-five, eighty. *Shift!* The wind got louder and the door seals whistled. Ninety. The fenders started shaking. *Shift!* The Hall-Scott was now in full roar. He could feel the tires expanding with speed, now blithely dancing over the rutted pavement. A few more seconds, and he was in the zone above the one-hundred mark on the speed-ometer, a place where the numbers ended because once you got there, it was all academic. It might as well have been marked "Insanity" or "Goodbye." The engine rumbled and screamed. An unfortunate rabbit met its demise, spattering some remains on the windshield. Nick hit the washer switch. The wipers wouldn't stay in contact with the glass at this speed. Too much wind. Still nothing in the mir-rors. The truck started to sway with speed as the wind howled. He took a gently sweeping turn to the left. Up ahead, the high beams illuminated a dark-ened sign: "Happy Navajo Acres Family Funland! Rest a Spell! Dinosaur on Rock Only Five Cents!" A delighted-looking freckled all-American boy of about 10 smiled, wearing an Indian headdress and drinking a Coke on the billboard welcoming visitors. It was a pitiful little roadside attraction a few miles outside of Ash Fork. He knew there was a place to park behind the main barn that would shield the truck from traffic passing on 66.

He lifted the throttle, and the truck seemed to decelerate like it had a parachute behind it. In truth, the trailer was basically just about as aerodynamic as a parachute. He applied the brakes and started to downshift. He watched the meter showing the air reserve for the brakes quickly descend as pistons pressed acres of asbestos against the massive steel drums. He reached down and killed the lights. There was a three-quarter moon not yet entirely obscured by the incoming clouds. It would be light enough. Finally down to a safe speed, he made a quick right on a gravel path, passing the darkened shapes of some fiberglass bison and jocular Indians holding tomahawks and bows. A giant arrow projected out of the ground. He made a right at the barn that held the snake exhibit and General Pershing's original boots from the Pancho Villa days. He stopped the truck. He remembered he needed to leave the engine running to keep the turbo from cooking the oil in its own bearings. If anyone asked, he was just stopping for the night. Not enough rest time back in Flag. Gotta think safety.

He reached into the glovebox, grabbed his flashlight and found the keys for the heavy padlocks on the trailer door. He slid down to the ground and started walking back to the trailer.

And then, the dead spot . . .

He stopped at the midway point of the trailer. He looked around. Things were looking small. "OK, OK, OK," he kept saying. He breathed deeply. He looked up at the tractor in its almost-glowing redness. It seemed to be shrinking and coming into sharper focus. The exhaust pipe on the driver's side was glowing a cherry red near where it emerged from beneath the truck. The Hall-Scott was still chuffing away. There was no one else around -- not a living, visible creature in the juniper-dotted high-desert scrub.

Looming above the truck and the barn was a towering totem pole. It wasn't the kind found among local tribes, but rather what people in new Chevy and Plymouth station wagons full of cranky eight-year-olds expected to see at an Indian theme park. The topmost figure in the totem was a stern eagle head. It stared down at him with deep concern.

Nick shook his head, then rubbed his temple with the flashlight.

"I am aware. I am aware. I am Nick Pente. I am of Greek descent. I play the guitar. I am from Chicago. I like egg salad and tomato. I watch Ed Sullivan when I can. I am—" He started to breathe more consciously. And he thought about Shelby.

He turned and fixed his gaze at the end of the trailer. Then, forced himself to start walking.

He got to the back and tried not to think at all. He wasn't curious. He wasn't. This was all an accident. It wasn't even Nick himself doing this. It was someone else. That's right. Someone who was not Nick put the key in the padlock. An unseen hand turned the key. The lock fell to the ground. Some mysterious force like the wind god Aeolus must have lifted the sliding door. It rolled up and disappeared above him with a thud.

Something turned the flashlight on and pointed it at the cargo, encased in a bunch of cardboard boxes. All those boring little cardboard boxes lashed to pallets and secured with straps to the internal slats along the walls of the trailer.

Nick smiled and shook his head. He let himself exhale with a sigh. It would have been so much more rewarding had it been a row of test tubes or the bulbous outline of a Mark 4 nuclear bomb or even a row of missiles. Boxes. The kind that look like they hold typing paper. What a great reward for his curiosity! Shelby had done nothing but incite the same sort of paranoia in him that was ripping the country apart. He was told it was paper products and, well, there you go, there was a "Continental Paper" logo stenciled on each box. He stepped up to grab the door handle. This had all been more paranoid bullshit...

Then he chanced to look at one of the boxes more closely. He realized that besides the "Continental Paper" stencil, each box also bore the terminal descriptor of "ARG," for Argonne Labs, then the terminal marking "PMO" for Pomona. All of that was well and good. But then, a few lines down were three letters separated by blank spaces, followed by four numerals. He was still smiling at himself and his silliness. He was chuckling. He read the letters out loud, and, slowly his laughter dissipated:

"N...K...D."

Images of Shelby at the Heartland and Troy from the Jet flashed in his mind.

"N...K...D."

Every box was marked "NKD1256."

"*NKD . . . knockout . . .*"

✳ ✳ ✳

Twenty minutes later, Nick was bringing the truck to a stop at the pumps at the Texaco station in Seligman, Arizona.

Usually, the station was open at all hours, with an attendant trundling out to offer fuel and service. This time, however, the lights were on and buzzing, but no one was home. There was a sign in the window with "back in 5 minits" scribbled on it in felt-tip pen. Nick was going to need fuel, but more than that, he needed to talk to someone. He looked up and down the road. An old Ford pickup rumbled by, going toward Flagstaff. There were goats in the bed. They bleated as the truck rolled along, and then were gone. The snow had started to fall. There was no sign of the Mercury.

Nick quickly walked across the concrete apron and the gravel lot to a telephone booth snugged up to the little cafe, which was now closed. He looked both ways, zipping up his jacket as he walked. He closed the door behind him and picked up the receiver and dialed a zero. There was an almost unbearable pause. He heard some clicking.

"Hello. Operator," came the nasally voice, finally.

"Yes, operator, I need to make a person-to-person collect call. Mission 6-1256 in San Francisco, California."

"Checking for that number now, sir." There was a little static on the line. "Whom do you wish to speak to at this number, sir?"

"I need to talk to a George Hunter White, please. Tell him it's important."

"And whom shall I say is calling?"

"Nick Pente, with Continental Paper."

A long minute passed, then the line was full of a gruff, street-hardened voice on the other end.

"Nick, what's going on?"

"George, this is Nick, Nick Pente in 201. Hey, I need to let you know, I think I'm being followed. Two guys in a black Mercury. It makes no sense, but there it is. You told me to call if I thought something was up. No idea what these guys might want with paper, and by the way, have you heard anything about some kind of dope called—"

George grumbled. "OK, what makes you think—"

"George, I just know it, OK? They were in Amarillo, they were in New Mexico, they were following me all across 66 from Flagstaff. I'm pretty sure I saw them in Flagstaff. It's dark. I can't be sure."

"OK, hold on. You said a black Mercury?"

"Yes, black. Looks like a '55. I think. Two-door. I can't see the plate."

"What do these guys look like?"

Nick described them. George told him to hold on. There was the muffled sound of voices in the background and shuffling. It took two or three agonizing minutes. Nick looked all around outside the phone booth. Then, George was back.

"OK, buddy, listen. I'm having someone check on that car." Then he interrupted himself. "But first, tell me." It sounded like he was taking a drink.

"How you feelin'? How's the job workin' out for you? You feelin' all right? I know it's early for you, but then you guys work all night, I know."

Nick was slightly confused. "Well, yeah. I'm doing fine. I mean, everything's fine, just a normal milk run. Well, except for these guys."

"Let me ask you this. You uh...takin' anything to stay awake out there? Like NoDoz or some pills or somethin'?"

"No, George, just a lot of coffee. I drive for fourteen and rest for ten. Sometimes, I drive a bit longer, if I have tire problems. That's enough. You wanna see my log book? Should I mail it? It's just like the ICC says it should be."

"OK, well, give me a second here. I'm glad to hear that because I know a lot of drivers out there are on the reds and the bennies, I mean, just trying to make some dough. Can't blame 'em, really. You know, times is tough. I really feel for the little guy out there. Economy's in the shitter, that's what they say. It's enough to make a guy want to go into government work or something. So, black Mercury, like a '55 or so?"

Nick could have sworn George was stalling. He was talking slowly, with a lot of pauses. Maybe he was drunk. He heard glasses clinking in the background and something that almost sounded like a girl's giggle. A hand went over the receiver and off again. There was a rustling sound.

Finally, George came back and had a more direct tone. "OK, Nick. Start headin' west on 66. We have some agents, *err, company employees,* I mean, in Kingman. That's like seventy-five miles. Less than an hour, if you're doing it right. But look, I am going to call ahead and have them meet you in—where is that? Where? OK, Peach Springs. There's a town called Peach Springs. That's like halfway. They'll help you out. Look for two guys in a red Dodge, I think it is. Dodge or Plymouth. One of the new ones with the fins and shit. Look, this is real important. Do not let them guys get that truck, OK? Them guys who's following you. Yah hear me? Don't let them touch that load. I'm relying on you here, buddy." There was a palpable tension in his voice.

"OK. Peach Springs. Thirty-seven miles. I can do it in less than half an hour." Nick turned around and noticed that the attendant was back and had started filling up the truck.

"Yeah, Pente. Haul ass to Peach Springs. Don't let them touch it. Oh, and remember, *safety first.*"

"I know, thanks." Nick hung up the phone and turned to leave the booth.

But the door wouldn't open.

He looked up from the handle and into the face of the larger of the two men from the Jet. He was holding the door from the outside. Nick looked at him. The man smiled that little sickening half-smile he recognized from before. Nick shuddered. The shorter of the two men was there as well. His acne looked like it had gotten worse in the last day. He had his right hand in the pocket of his jacket and wore a totally bland expression. It made the small slits he had for eyes all the more apparent. The circular fluorescent light of the phone booth buzzed above them. The Texaco station gleamed in the distance, its lights illuminating the truck and the pavement around it. Snowflakes fell past the glow of the canopy.

The tall man allowed the door to open slowly. He was actually the one opening it, Nick feeling no urgency to hasten the encounter from inside. Now he was face to face with this tall man in a homburg, who smiled coldly, quizzically. Nick could almost smell his breath. He stood silently. Over his shoulder, Nick could see the old Texaco attendant in his coveralls sliding the gas nozzle into the truck. The pump soon began to make the *ding-ding-ding* sound and a repetitive squeak as the gallons poured into the tank.

The tall man opened his mouth. "I have a message for you," he said slowly, in an accent that sounded like a mixture of German and Slavic. There was a strange *"ich"* sound when he said "message."

"And you," he continued. "you have the key." The man extended his hand slowly and opened his palm, creepily.

Nick's hands were starting to tingle. He was fighting the urge to see things in miniature. Mentally, he tried telling himself something about himself—something to increase his awareness. "I am aware. I am Nick Pente. I am of Greek descent. I am...I am..." It wasn't working as well as he had hoped. He was being pulled down by the dead spot, slowly and inexorably.

"You have the key. The key, for the message," said the man, offering a trade. Nick's mind was racing. There was something familiar in the man's voice, which was soothing, smooth, almost bland in its menace. The way he said "message" and "key" reminded Nick of something. He couldn't put his finger on it. It was something reminding him about Chicago and about darkness. A darkened room. A door. A door with a window. Script on the window. Something about some taste on his tongue. Thick fingers. Flashing lights. A white face. Words repeated again and again. Aware. Aware.

Then, something happened, something Nick had almost forgotten could originate in him. It didn't occur to him it was a risk. He wasn't on guard against it. He looked at the man's face. The combination of the gray hair visible just beneath the line of his hat and the ice-blue eyes and the foreign accent suddenly reminded him of someone he had known very briefly -- thirteen years before.

"So you want the key, huh?" asked Nick. His voice had dropped into deep breathiness, hollow, calm and yet crazed. He felt a small grin coming over him as his chest tightened. The man nodded but seemed surprised at Nick's response. His eyes shifted. His companion's eyes narrowed even further. The man looked like he was going to repeat his words yet again.

A voice rang out from near the pumps. "Hey, mister! You on account with us here?" The homburg man's stare broke off. Nick slammed the door open the rest of the way with full-force. It caught the large man's left hand and forearm. He gasped in pain. Nick braced himself against the opposite side of the booth, and his right fist connected with the man's head just near his temple. The man groaned, grasping to get his arm out of the folding door. Nick pulled it back then slammed it again, moving out toward the man. His young companion had been caught by surprise but had come around behind him. Nick struck the man again, trying to hit his jaw but getting his cheek instead. The next punch hit the door. The glass shattered. He pulled his hand back in pain; blood and glass shards covered it. He saw the flash of what looked like a blade. Nick grasped the upper edge of the phone booth and swung out, kicking the larger man in the chest and sending him sprawling, knocking the younger one down as he fell. Nick ran out across the concrete apron toward the truck. Nick started remembering an old friend of his, and in a way, he realized he had begun to channel him. As he ran, he heard himself shouting, *"That's the key, you fucking kraut!"*

By the time Nick reached the truck, he had pulled the truck's key out of his pocket and was ready to open the door, but the gas nozzle was still in the tank. He grabbed it and ripped it out, splashing gas on his trousers in the process. Gas spilled on the pavement. Nick got the door open and tossed himself inside, starting the engine almost in a single motion. He looked through the windshield and saw the long drawn-out face of the attendant, who was stretched across the hood and trying to clean the rabbit guts off. He looked like Buster Keaton. *"Get off my fucking truck!"* Nick screamed. The Hall-Scott roared to life. As the attendant slid to the ground and leapt to the gas pump, Nick looked in the mirrors and caught the sight of the two men running toward the cab. He revved the enormous engine and slammed into first gear. Dropping the clutch, the turbo screamed as all tires on both rear axles spun, even under the weight of the load. The truck lurched forward, leaving the men tumbling behind it just as they had tried to grasp the grab-rails near the sleeper cab. Second gear engaged with a grind. No time to double-clutch.

With a lurch across the gravel shoulder, he was back on 66 and headed toward Peach Springs. He heard the turbocharger spooling up as he zoomed toward redline in each of the ten gears, and each time it did, there was a tremendous forward lurch. He was revving the Hall-Scott out in every gear.

Nick was a few blocks away from the Texaco when he glanced into his mirrors to see the Mercury swinging out of the parking lot, the attendant running behind it from the island of light in the dark down. Nick continued to accelerate. He could see the snow in the beams of the truck's lights. If he could get the Diamond-T up to its maximum speed, he would likely lose the two men or at least get the attention of a state trooper. It was only thirty-seven miles to Peach Springs. Seligman started to fade in his mirrors.

Nick was likely going a little over ninety when he found that the overpass had iced up.

As he approached the midpoint, the truck's tail started to edge to the right. He overcorrected, and the trailer whipped him back the other way. The whole rig was sliding. Faster than he could react, the tractor was over the concrete sidewall, listing toward its left side and then slamming itself back down as the cab knocked out post after post of the guardrail, making a horrible graunching sound as it skated along, driven by the momentum of the trailer. The trailer was pushing it with tons of pressure. Gradually, almost miraculously, it ground to a halt.

The tractor hung directly over the railroad tracks beneath him. His body slammed forward to meet the wheel, his chest thrust against the Diamond-T logo in its center.

Nick jerked himself up from the surface of the bed. He gasped. Euri was on top of him, moaning, her pert breasts bouncing with rhythm as she rode, grinding herself against him. He felt himself deep inside of her warm tightness. She growled. He moaned and started thrusting upward. She fell forward and pressed her tongue into his mouth as she grabbed his hair.

12

Pahana

"Someday, you will meet him"
"But when?"
"You will know. You will know."
"How?"

Hehewuti was holding a piece of bone between her lips. Her fingers deftly stroked through Euri's hair. Each stroke hurt just a little bit, but Euri was used to it by now. She knew it was worth it. She had seen her reflection in the glass and in the still ponds. She wanted this.

"You will know. I knew I was to be with your father. No one could tell me. I just knew."

"Will he be Hopi?"

"I don't know, Euri. No one knows." Hehewuti knew this conversation would continue, so she gave the bone fragment to Euri to hold so she was better able to enunciate the words she had said so many times before. This, too, was a gesture of love.

"Euri, I don't know. Hopi men, they are different. They are different from your father. They are farmers. And they weave. Your father weaves because I told him to weave. He never did before."

"What's wrong with weaving?" asked Euri.

"Nothing. Nothing at all. He raises sheep. He loves sheep. They make wool. He weaves rugs. It's fine. But Hopi men, they—"

"So, why should I..."

"Euri, you are not..." Hehewuti was getting impatient, but only a little. Euri hadn't washed her hair in a while. It made it both easier and harder.

"Euri, you are Bacho's daughter, and you are my daughter. Do you know what that means?"

Euri could think of a few things it meant, but didn't know the proper response in this case.

"It means you are *you*. And Euri must wait for someone special. Someone who understands. Do you understand me?"

"Yes."

"You are the daughter of the Hard Mother of the West, and Bacho, the Coyote. He comes from different blood. Your grandmothers don't want to know your father. They let him marry me because I told them I would marry him."

"But you don't know who I will marry?"

"No. You have to find him. And he won't be...oh, Euri." Hehewuti held Euri's chin and turned Euri's face toward her. "Life is never easy for our people. It's even harder for you and me."

She smiled. Euri smiled back.

"You need to wait. Wait for the man who tells you of the places he's been. It will be like you have been there as well, by his side. Take that man. Follow him. He is that man. He is your husband."

She turned Euri's head back so she could finish the right-side whorl.

"Is he Pahana?"

"I don't know."

"Pahana has been everywhere."

"I don't know."

"Pahana is wonderful."

"He is," said Hehewuti. Then, thoughtfully, "If he exists."

Euri started, then tried to turn her head. Hehewuti held her chin in place. She kept working on the whorl.

"Euri, you must promise me," said Hehewuti, her fingers still dancing through Euri's hair. "You must promise me to not go with a man because he says he is Pahana. Pahana will come. But he will never, never, never do one thing. He will never say he is Pahana."

"But, he will wear red, right?"

"Perhaps, child. Perhaps." Hehewuti moved her stool to the other side of the chair and started running her fingers through Euri's hair, separating it into strands.

And so she sat there, hearing her mother hum a song while her fingers interlaced the strands of hair and pulled them over the bone. Euri thought about what Hehewuti had said about life being hard for them—especially for them. She thought about her life as the sole offspring of the Hard Mother of the West and her father, the Coyote. She thought about the stories her father had told her about the old days of the people, the ones who had gone before, the ones Bacho himself said he represented as the last remnant. And in the back of her mind she decided then that if she were ever to marry, it would need to be to Pahana. Pahana himself alone would suffice. And when Pahana arrived, she would return to the East with him to learn all that he knew—to see it for herself. Knowing through him wouldn't be enough. If Pahana didn't arrive, she would die a spinster, never having left the valley and her mother and father. And as she sat there, the occasional tugs against her scalp strengthened her resolve the way little darts of pain can at times. The weaving went on, accompanied by the humming.

"There, Euri. That is beautiful. My beautiful girl." Hehewuti pulled back to admire her craft.

Then, there was a knock on the door. It opened. Two men were standing in the doorway, smiling, nervous. One held a Bible. The other held a gun. Hehewuti pulled Euri close to her. Euri looked out the window to see a man she recognized walking towards the shack. He was a white man in a cowboy duster.

13

Enzymes

When Nick awoke, he was alone. Soft sunlight illuminated the interior of the shack. He heard the sheep outside. He got up and pulled on his pants. His shirt – the one with the red piping on the shoulders --was hanging on the bedpost. He grasped it and put it on. It took away some of the chill.

He walked outside. Bacho was in the field tending to the sheep. Euri had been crouching near the fire, cooking. She saw him and stood up, then turned back to what she was doing. She was wearing her hair down for the first time he had seen. It was gathered into a ponytail behind her. He walked to her side.

"Good morning. Breakfast," she said cheerfully, scraping some eggs and mutton out of the cast-iron skillet and onto a tin plate for him. She had a different mood, a different attitude than what he had seen before. She still exuded warmth, but it was a lower flame that seemed to fully involve her, as though her embers had suffused with a glow. She seemed self-consciously dutiful where she had been frivolous before. She squeezed Nick's shoulder and went back to cooking.

The rest of the day, Bacho went about his domestic duties, and so Nick did with Euri. They would see him in the distance, mending the fence, feeding the animals, tending to more sheep while they gathered wood and talked and made plans.

"When did he get back?"

"I don't know. He woke me up with noise, working outside," said Euri.

"Did he say anything?" asked Nick.

"No, but he didn't need to."

As they worked together, there was a new tenderness between them, something more like familiarity. Nick's hands casually squeezed her hips as he walked by. She would rub his shoulder. Once he found himself standing behind her at the well. He wondered if Bacho could see as he pondered indulging his senses with her again, there outside, like the animals. He wondered if Bacho would care. He wondered if it mattered.

Quietly, they started to make plans that would take them away from the farm to Chicago. Euri tried to conceal her excitement. Her responses were low and breathy and conspiratorial.

That night, Bacho sat with them at the fire. He was silent. He finished his meal and walked off in the distance again without saying a word. Once he disappeared, Nick and Euri fell into each other again, beside the fire. And again after that. And once more in the middle of the night when he awakened in bed next to her. Afterward, Nick walked outside. He wanted to see the stars. Euri had fallen back to sleep.

Nick stared up into the sky, pondering the millions of dots of light stretching out into infinity. He remembered Bacho saying all was made of stars, of stardust. And now, there was a new star in the heavens, one made by man. Nick's eyes scanned the clear skies, and he wondered if he could see it, and if he could, would it shine as brightly as those far off dots of light, millions of which might have already died, their light only then – that night -- getting to him on Earth? Would it have mattered to him if he had seen it? What did it mean that one of the miniscule dots in the heavens was a small metallic orb made by Russians and placed into an unstable orbit, destined to return to Earth in a fiery streak, soon to be extinguished? Why was that important?

He thought about how all that had happened to him in life, from his earliest memories to the still slightly enervated and winded feeling he had after his latest time with Euri not more than ten minutes before. Looking into the heavens, they existed all at once, in a single moment, as a single dot of light. Everything that had ever happened.

And, suddenly, he was back in Dr. Kultra's darkened office, five years before.

"The therapy has proven beneficial so far, *ja?*"

"Yes, Doc. I'm getting the feeling that I can handle things better now. I haven't had...a...an..."

"An episode?"

"I haven't had the dead spot recently, no. I've been thinking more of awareness, using the phrases you gave me. And the mirror work. I feel more attached...more secure."

"Good, good, good." Dr. Kultra smiled as he paused and cleared his throat, straightening his wide frame in his leather chair and smoothing his tie with both hands. "Tell me, Nick, have you ever had a test for your enzymes?"

"Well, Doc, I don't recall, unless they did that in the army."

"Oh, you left the army in 1946. Years ago! This is a very new test. Very recent. We are finding that digestive enzymes are very good indicators of overall psychiatric health. The test is painless and can be administered here. In fact, it only involves the placement of a small piece of paper on your tongue for a few moments. Then, we would like to keep you here for a few minutes to observe you. I would be assisted in observing you by a few of my students. Is that acceptable to you?"

"Well." Nick wondered. "You say it's a test, like a spit test?"

"Yes, the digestive enzymes present in your saliva. Yes." Dr. Kultra nodded.

"I need to be observed afterward? I don't think I've ever had a test like that. Don't they just usually send the samples somewhere?"

"As I said, Nick, this is a very new test. We can get results almost immediately. I would only like a few of my students to observe the test in progress, so they are familiar with administering it, and your reactions to the results. It's quite painless, I assure you. Shall I bring them in now?"

"I guess. If it will help."

"I am so happy you are cooperative! This is such a great step forward in your journey to greater awareness. You have moved beyond yourself. That is the message I give to you, you have the key. You hold the key in yourself." Dr. Kultra reached down to his intercom on his desk.

"Miss Sanders, please send in the students." He leaned back and smiled, slowly twirling his sideburns and nodding at Nick approvingly.

Three young people walked in, a woman and two men—probably all in their mid to late twenties. The young woman wore a tweed skirt and a sweater. The men were in slacks and dress shirts with ties.

"Students, this is Nick. Nick, this is Bob, Dennis, and Cheryl. They are graduate students in my program in psychology here at the university." Dr. Kultra nodded to each student, in order. They smiled and waved awkwardly as they laughed. All had textbooks and notebooks in their hands. Dr. Kultra picked up the microphone for his dictation machine.

"Mr. Nicholas Pente has come to me with assistance on a problem involving extreme anxiety manifesting in occasional catatonia. He says the problem originated in childhood. He suffered trauma during the war, which likely exacerbated the symptoms. He reports today that cognitive methods have shown some success. We are today testing him with a new methodology for certain digestive enzymes associated with his disorder. With the outcome of this test, we shall consult with the staff endocrinologists at the university hospital for their advice on further actions, if any. Now, Nick, this is very simple." Setting the microphone down, he pulled a small plastic box from inside his desk. He opened it slowly and carefully.

With a pair of tweezers, he pulled a piece of paper from the inside and held it up before Nick. It was red and wasn't quite as large as a postage stamp. He placed it on a glass petri dish in front of him. Reaching for a bottle with an eyedropper, he placed a single drop on the paper scrap. "And, now, we apply the activation solution. Here, first take a drink of water. That's good. Now, you simply place this on your tongue for one full minute, then open your mouth, and I will retrieve it with tweezers." Dr. Kultra leaned forward with the tweezers.

Nick looked at the Doctor and then at the students. Each of them had textbooks in their laps and spiral notebooks open before them, using the textbooks as a sort of desk. They smiled. Nick looked back at the doctor. "Are you comfortable, Nick?"

"I guess so."

"Then, shall we begin?"

Nick gulped. He opened his mouth, and the doctor carefully placed the paper on this tongue. Nick closed his mouth and gently placed his tongue against the roof of his mouth. The taste was neutral, or perhaps mildly salty, like a mild saline solution. He looked at Cheryl. She opened her fresh new notebook and started scribbling notes. She wasn't unattractive. The sweater fitted her form quite well, and the skirt was flattering. He looked at her flat belly falling and rising with her breath, noting her fulsome breasts beneath her sweater. His eyes traced down to the textbook in her lap. Just before he lost consciousness, he noticed the name "Stewart" etched in it roughly, in pencil. And then, all became white, for the blink of an eye.

He blinked, and when he opened his eyes, everything seemed the same, but the students were slouching, and the boys had loosened their ties. Bob was staring at him with what seemed a stricken expression. He noticed that Miss Stewart had written enough to have turned through about three quarters of her new notebook, and her skirt had inched up a little. Though it didn't seem like it had been a full minute, the doctor was ready.

"Very good, Mr. Pente! Very good. Here, open." He took the sample from Nick's tongue with the tweezers and scrutinized it, seeming to put an unusual amount of care into beholding the now purple piece of wet paper. "I see...students, can you see this? Very good." Dennis and Cheryl looked and nodded, their brows raised in a show of enthusiastic recognition. Bob still looked at Nick and seemed fixated until Dennis nudged him to look at the paper that the doctor now held above the desk in the fluorescent office light. "You see, Mr. Pente, perhaps this message holds the key to your condition."

"What's it look like?" asked Nick, expectantly, but still confused and a bit drowsy, though not drowsy.

"Oh, it's very, very good. The coloration is as expected." The doctor picked up his dictation microphone again. "Test completed as expected. I will forward this sample to the staff at the hospital. Initial results appear..." He paused and looked at Nick while nodding once, extending the word with a Teutonic trill of the letter *r* "norrrrmal." Cheryl giggled at his little self-jibe. The doctor smiled at her and continued. "However, I will need to recommend that Mr. Pente return to the office or the campus clinic monthly for monitoring purposes. This is very important, and that message is key. Yes." he paused. "That message...is key..."

Then, the doctor got to his feet and shook Nick's hand. The students shook his hand on his way out. Nick felt bewildered and very thirsty.

That visit marked the point at which the disturbing dreams stopped. Nick's dead spots slowly decreased in frequency. He continued his cognitive therapy with the doctor during weekly visits. A month later, he started training for his new career as a truck driver after the doctor proclaimed him "for most intents and purposes, cured." He did insist on continuing to monitor Nick for enzymes, though. Nick made time to drop by the clinic each month, doing so for five years.

Well, each month until the last. He missed that one, it again occurred to him.

But now, all of that seemed so far away. Now, he looked at the darkened mountains and how they were silhouetted against the fields of stars he could see from the farm. Whether made by man or by God, all was made of stars. And all was mortal, in a way.

And he was a star pondering other stars that, as far as he knew, only appeared to be there. He could tell the directions by the stars. He knew roughly which way he and Euri would need to go when they left the next day or the day after.

He hummed the Perry Como song again. Just a few bars, softly.

He went back to bed, spooning up behind Euri and softly cradling her breasts.

14

Real, Real Wrong?

The next day sometime after rising just as the sun was starting to illuminate the valley, Nick saw Bacho tending to the sheep at the far end of the clearing opposite the shack. He had started to shear them. T his meant that the weather would soon be warmer. Or, maybe he just needed wool. It was still cold outside. Nick walked toward him while Euri prepared breakfast.

Bacho knew how to shear sheep. It was lyrical, in a way, watching him work. There was a singularity to his motion. The sheep barely made a sound. Most seemed to be standing in line, waiting their turn.

Nick stood near him and watched. Bacho began to speak softly as he worked. "I went to the mountain, last night and the night before. It was cold. I talked and thought. My people, my fathers—they were not Hopi, and they were not Dineh. They were different. Euri and me. We all that's left. But we know of the Hopi ways. What they believe." Bacho bent to pick up another sheep. He flipped it on its back. The shears followed the line underneath and along its sides. The sheep didn't make a sound.

"Hopi, they believe in Pahana. Pahana is the lost white brother. He move to the east. He said he'd come back. When he come, there would be peace. Pahana knew all was one. He knew we all made of stars. So, he come back as teacher, as priest. Then, everyone happy. Death gone." He flipped the sheep over and started on its back with the shears.

"So, when I see you in the truck on the bridge, I saw you wear a shirt with red. Pahana supposed to wear red, they say. I never believed Hopi ways before. They nice people. They have sheep. But I don't believe in their ways. Until I see you.

"I bring you here because I think you maybe Pahana. You bring stories of fighting in war, but you are peaceful. You tell of death and hate, but you love Euri. I think you good to marry Euri. You drive machines and shoot guns, but you gather water and wood with your hands with me. I start thinking, maybe you Pahana. Maybe Hopi is right." Bacho started on the sheep's face.

"But now, you talk to Euri and decide to leave. You go back east to Chicago. You leave to the east again." He finished the sheep. "And you take my little girl." With that, he slapped the sheep lightly on its hind end and sent it away.

"So, now I think maybe you not Pahana after all, or Hopi wrong. Real, real wrong." Bacho paused, slightly winded.

Nick looked at Bacho. Then his gaze moved out to the mountains surrounding the valley. He looked back down at the ground—at the wool that had just been shorn. "Bacho," he began. "I love your daughter. She's everything I could want, everything I've needed since I was a baby. I'm the man who loves your daughter. I'm not Pahana. I love living here, and I love the things you've taught me. I honor you like a father, the father I should have had. But Euri is young and has dreams. I can't let her stay here on this farm—not now that I've learned what she knows and what she wants to know. She needs to see the world. She could never be happy here after..."

Bacho looked up at him from his knees. "After *you*, no. After what you tell her, no."

Nick fumed. He looked around, gathering his thoughts. "Bacho, look. I have been here how long? A few weeks, maybe? Just a few weeks. She showed me her books. Who brought her the books? How long has she had them?" Bacho's eyes darted at him.

"Missionary. Christian man brought her Bible."

"No, the others. All those others under the floor." Bacho looked down. "You mean to tell me you brought her those books for her whole life, books about everything, and knew she was reading them all, and I come along, and I'm the one who poisoned her mind? In what. . . *three weeks?* For Chrissakes, Bacho, she's read *Madame Bovary!*" Nick's body stiffened. He fumed as he turned away in disgust.

Bacho looked off in the distance.

"Some missionaries, Christian men. They tried to take her books. They told her was sin. Some missionary say was ok. Others, they tried to take those books I give her. They say read only Bible. To me, just more books. Euri learn from them. Not too important. So, we hide books. And..." Bacho went silent. His hands were moving through the grass around him. His gaze moved around the valley and up to the tops of the eastern peaks.

Nick still needed to get his point across. "Look, this is what I am saying. You love her very much. You made sure she was educated. You brought her books. You let her read. When you read a book— when anyone reads a book—they want to see what the book describes. They want to see it for themselves. So, I show up and can tell her what England and France and the Field Museum look like. Do you see what I am saying? You brought me here, Bacho. I wanted to leave at first. But, instead, I stayed – because you wanted me to -- and I became the biggest book of all for Euri. And now, she wants to go with me back to my world."

Bacho still gazed off in the distance. He looked at the sky. He looked eastward toward the San

Francisco Peaks near Flagstaff. He looked down again. Slowly, tears welled up in his eyes. Nick didn't know what to do. He wanted to comfort him. He didn't know how he would take it. Nick put his hand on his shoulder. He felt the hard muscle underneath the plaid shirt. It felt like concrete.

Nick thought back on the time he had spent with Bacho. He had begun to feel attached to him, despite this amusing idea of his that he was some sort of visiting Hopi god from the east. It was a craziness that he indulged. Bacho had become like a stand-in for his own father, and as Nick looked at the scene that surrounded him, his affection for the place and for Bacho tugged at him. Still, he thought back on Euri. Her eyes – those flashing, angry, almost contemptuous eyes. They suddenly appeared before him in his imagination. And then her words rang again in his ears:

They were in a bubble. They made a decision. It was time to go.

"Bacho," said Nick, pausing to take a deep breath. "We're leaving in the morning." With that, Nick turned and started walking toward the shack.

Bacho called out after him. "Tomorrow the day of the low sun. Bad day to travel. You should wait."

Nick kept walking. It was time for breakfast.

15

The Two Tapestries

The sun rose late the next day, and Nick had gathered that it was December 21, the day of the low sun: the solstice. He recalled things from books and movies about how some cultures saw it was a day of reckoning or something. T o him, it meant only that he was a few days older than thirty-two years, and as he stretched out in bed beside Euri, he felt every one of them. He got to his feet and stoked the fire in the stove. Bacho wasn't around.

The front door opened with a squeak. The skies were overcast, and the wind had started to blow, softly at first. The clouds touched the tops of the mountains. There was a sparse mantle of white on the peaks already visible just beneath the clouds. He shut the door.

By now, Euri was stirring. He leaned down and warmly kissed her lips. She opened her beautiful eyes again and smiled. They seemed to gaze into each other's souls.

"Today's the day," he whispered in her ear.

"We get to Chicago?" she said expectantly as she stretched, though it was really more of a tease.

"No, no, no. That will take a few more days once we get back to Seligman. But it's a start." Nick rubbed her fulsome hips. "And the most important step..."

"Of any journey is the first," she said with him in unison. They laughed and kissed again.

"I think it's the last step. That saying is wrong!" Euri said.

"What do you mean?"

"I just want to get there. I want the trip over." She laughed.

"But the journey is the experience. That's the good part!"

She shook her head.

"Ahh, youthful impatience. That's what you have. You're young."

She blushed and smiled in a naughty way. "You shut up, Nick Pente. Fuck you."

Nick gasped, then realized that some of the books Bacho had brought her had more colorful vocabulary than others.

"You little...bitch..." Nick grabbed her and pushed her down on the bed, tickling and laughing with her. He came to rest between her legs.

Their departure would be delayed by at least a few minutes.

The night before, they had bundled the things they thought they would need in two bags. Nick would carry the leather knapsack that had once contained books but was now stocked with some food and two sheepskin botas filled with water. Euri had clothes and a few keepsakes in a bundle she would strap to her back. She had wanted to bring several books along, but Nick bargained her down to only two: the Zane Grey book they had read to each other and a picture book showing some contents of museums around the world, including the Field Museum in Chicago. Euri had suggested he bring *Paradise Lost,* but after he scanned a few pages of the book, it brought back too many memories. Or associations.

Euri sat on the bed and looked around her. She was mentally preparing herself to leave. As she sat there in silence, Nick thought he could hear her speaking under her breath. He imagined it was a prayer, though Euri didn't seem religious at all. It distinguished her from her father, though Bacho's piety itself seemed more formal and traditional than it was deeply felt as a faith—except as concerted Hehewuti.

Nick peeked outside. The winds had gotten higher, whipping up dust and causing the sheep to gather for warmth. A few more of them had been shorn.

"Are you ready?" he asked her.

She paused, looked into his eyes, and said, "Yes." She smiled. He took her hand.

The door swung open. It was Bacho. He wore the ceremonial costume. It was one Nick recognized from when he was chanting over his legs, but the mask was missing. In its place, he had painted his face with a wild assortment of stripes, dots, and colors. The colors were white, red, and black. He wore a look of agitation and excitement Nick had never seen on him before. He took a bold stance in the doorway. The wind blew behind him, stirring up dust and some sparse snowflakes. Nick stepped back. Euri took Nick's arm.

Bacho held a small leather sack in one hand, closed with a drawstring. While keeping his eyes on Nick, he stepped into the house. He turned toward the doorway and reached into the bag and pulled out a handful of cornmeal. He leaned down and filtered out a line of cornmeal across the threshold of the doorway, which wasn't really a transom, but more like just the part of the raw wood floor that allowed wind and dirt to filter into the shack under the door. He stood up and turned, again staring at Nick.

"Bad day to travel. You must stay. There is work to be done. Not all work done for me. Very important you stay," he said slowly and deliberately, and then stood in silence.

Nick looked at Euri, who had an expression of near embarrassment.

"*Atzchee*" she said, softly. "I'm a married woman now. I will go with Nick, my husband, to Chicago."

Bacho's stare moved off to a point beyond her somewhere. "Bad day to travel. The sun is low. It the day of the low sun," he said calmly, exuding an air of self-restraint.

Nick looked at his savagely decorated face. He would try to seek some middle ground with the man in the war paint. "Bacho, the weather is getting bad out there, but I think it will get better as we go down the mountain. Would you like to come with us? To guide us?"

Bacho glared at him. "*No!*" He seemed to stamp his foot. "I stay here! This is my land! My family land! Euri is my family!" Then, he switched to his native language, and Euri responded, softly at first, then louder. Nick looked at her. The strand of adamantine resolve was blazing across her features. Bacho was gesticulating broadly, waving the sack of cornmeal as he spoke. He and Euri shouted at each other. Euri held Nick's arm tightly, flexing her grip while pointing at her father with the other hand.

Nick's hands started to feel funny. And he started to feel his perspective on the room changing. He said to himself, silently, "I am Nick Pente; I am from Chicago; I am of Greek descent, son of an optician, and I am aware."

He started to remember a night sixteen years before, in a row house in Chicago's South Side. His father was standing in front of him. That night, Nick's legs were weak, and his throat was dry. A tremor rose up his spine and seemed to make his head shake. He was fighting off the dead spot harder than he had ever before. His father, a balding man of about forty, stood before him in that dimly lit hallway. He wore a striped bathrobe, the same one he had worn for as long as Nick could remember.

"Nicky, where do you think you're going at this hour?"

"Out for a while to meet the guys next door." His throat went dry. His hands were feeling strange to him. His father placed the round spectacles he had been cleaning back on his face and saw Nick's book bag slung on one shoulder over the wool coat he had gotten for his sixteenth birthday a few days before. His father harrumphed.

"Nicky, what do you have in mind? Really?" Nick looked away. "Is this what I think it is? You're sixteen. You're still in school." He was getting agitated. Words were getting more strained.

"Dad, Rob Hanson joined up already. Two days ago."

"You're a sophomore. You need to finish school."

"Rob was only a junior, and he's just sixteen."

"He'll be dead in a few weeks." His dad's voice trailed off, and he swallowed hard.

"Nah, he's strong. He's going to be OK. We talked about it. He's going to—"

"Nicky, I need you to stay here. You're all I've got. Anyway, what are you going to tell them at the medical exam about your problem with..." He pulled his glasses from his head again and wiped them on his robe. "Your little blackouts?"

Nick stared back at him.

Suddenly, Nick was back in the shack with Euri and Bacho yelling at each other. Bacho had taken to stamping one foot on the floorboards as he yelled, making the whole place shake. The trap door under the rug started to bounce, forcing its outline into the starry rug that concealed it above.

Euri switched back to English. "Nick is my husband. I love you, father, but I must go. We must go." Her tone was urgent and pleading.

Bacho was furious. "I not leave my land! You not leave our land! Nobody left! Just you and me! This is our land! This all we got!"

Euri looked at him, and after a pause, her tone suddenly changed to viperous indignation. She flailed out with venom, her lips pulled tight against her teeth, seething. Growling at first, she shouted a few words in the language she and her father shared, and when her father heard them, he stopped. He looked shocked. He straightened up for a moment, and then shifted his weight, disconsolately. He looked defeated.

Then, the other origin of the iron resolve that showed so much in his daughter became clear. He lunged for her throat. Euri grabbed his hands and tried to scream. Nick stepped forward and grabbed Bacho by the shoulders. He pulled hard. Bacho ignored him as his hands sank into his daughter's neck. His teeth were clenched. He growled. For an old man, he was incredibly strong. He started slamming her head against the bedpost as he yelled. Nick looked at Euri and saw an expression of panic and pain. Nick moved his feet to get better leverage. He put his feet behind Bacho's legs, slammed his knees into his thighs and yanked him back. Bacho stumbled toward the wall with more force than Nick intended. Before he hit the wall, he knocked over the rug loom. His head hit the windowsill, making the entire structure of the shack tremble, knocking out a few of the panes of mica glass. He slid to the floor, limp.

Shocked, Nick took a step back, then raced to Bacho's side. Euri screamed, her hands on her neck, but only once, then went silent. Nick patted Bacho's face. His head didn't turn. His eyes were still open, and his neck was limp. Nick felt for a carotid pulse, but found none. He had seen this enough for a whole year as he went from village to village in Normandy, around Paris, in Alsace, and after he crossed the Ruhr. He knew what it looked like. He took his thumb and forefinger and closed Bacho's eyes. He frowned and patted him on his iron shoulder. The excitement of the event stopped him from feeling much of anything right then.

Euri was standing near the bed, chanting something under her breath. Nick moved to her, but she turned away from him. He didn't know what to do. "Euri...I...He looked back at Bacho's lifeless form against the wall. He tried not to think that everything in his life had suddenly, with one misplaced use of excessive force, been destroyed. He thought back on the way Euri's face looked with her father's grip on her throat. He remembered the deep rage, the white-hot searing anger, the drive he felt to just do something, anything, to make it stop. He would have willed nothing different if Bacho had been strangling Nick himself. He didn't mean to kill him. He just wanted it to stop. He thought back on the German thirteen years before, the one with the mortar. That wasn't the same. It wasn't the same as this. He wanted that guy dead. He wanted him gone. He thought back on the conversation with Bacho near the fire that night he suggested Euri leave with him. Maybe it was true. Maybe all he was, was death. He looked at Bacho, a thin trail of blood leaking out of his nose, adding another shade of red to the paint on his face. Nick moved over to look at him again. Bacho: a friend. He had killed not only his wife's father, but also a friend, a man who had saved him. A man who had brought him to a happiness he didn't know existed, much less that he would have ever deserved.

Aye, maybe that was the rub.

As he stood over Bacho, his eyes moved to the loom. It lay fallen forward, revealing a rug that had been stored behind the one Bacho had been weaving. It was facedown on the back of the loom. Nick picked it up at an edge. He looked at it. It was about three by four feet.

The detail of the rug was fascinating. In fine threads, each shape had a shading and fineness to it that made it very vivid, as though carved in low relief. At first, the shapes seemed only fine and perhaps abstract. Then, Nick looked more closely.

The first scene in the upper left-hand corner showed the skyline of a big city, one that looked strangely familiar to Nick. Next to the skyline was a picture of a young couple and a baby. The father was holding the baby, and the mother stood to the side. In the frames that followed, a child was shown growing, playing with other children.

A few frames later, the child appeared with a larger figure, one wearing priest-like garb—whose hand seemed to be placed between the legs of the child.

Nick froze. Memories swirled. Years and years ago. A summer camp near a lake in Winnetka. The tubby face of a man above him, folds of fat under his chin. He wore a red robe. Sweat dripping from his temples, the man's lip quivering. The soft, wheezing voice pleading with him, trying to encourage him, confessing pleasure to him, asking if he felt pleasure as well. Sweating hands . . .

Nick gulped. His breath almost left him. His eyes raced across the rest of the tapestry. The father and son standing beside a bed. The mother always to the side in any group setting. A basketball court. A car. A depiction of war. A confrontation between the father and son, soldiers in training. A boat. More war. A figure beating another with something that looked like a gun. A jubilant return. The father and mother in graves. A man alone, sitting, walking, always alone, to the side of a group. A man lying on a couch while another man sat in a chair. A truck.

And the truck hanging off a bridge, about to intersect with a train below.

Nick's heart had almost stopped. He wheezed for breath. He looked at Euri. She had taken to swaying back and forth as she chanted, tears streaming down her cheeks.

Nick picked up the loom. He looked at the work that was still on it.

This was a tapestry of the same shape and size as the first, in just as great detail. It showed a man on a travois being dragged by another man in a hat. It showed them going up a mountain. It showed two figures—one male and one female—standing over a third reclining in bed. The three figures sat around a campfire and then worked on the farm, surrounded by sheep. It showed the female figure and one of the males in sexual union, then holding hands. It showed them working together for a few frames. Then, they stood over the third figure, who now had x's on his eyes. The remaining male figure stood over the corpse in a stance of pride. Then, the male and female figures were descending a mountain and walking in the desert, then approaching a road.

At that point, the threads left off. The tapestry was a few inches short of being complete on its bottom-right edge.

Everything was there—Everything. Things Nick had never told anyone. Things he hadn't remembered himself for decades. Repressed memories. *Things that had only happened in the last few minutes.* It was a complete picture of his life, but for the troubling omission of that last panel.

Nick's eyes turned toward Bacho again. His head had tilted further sideways. Blood flowed out from his right nostril. It had started to cover his ceremonial costume.

Nick looked at the tapestries.

Was this the message? Was this the key?

"Euri, we need to leave. We need to leave right now," he said, still staring at the tapestry. His voice was barely audible over the sound of the wind outside, which had increased in just the last few seconds. Nick turned to look at her. She lifted her tear-stained eyes to his. Euri looked back at her father. Something was pulling back at her, but her gaze suddenly hardened. She rose and walked to where the loom lay on the floor and pulled up the dusty sheepskin. The wind blew snowflakes through the missing windowpanes and onto Bacho. She placed the sheepskin over her father and kissed him on his head.

Nick picked up her bag and slowly took her hand. At first, it seemed she wouldn't move. She was limp and barely standing. She looked at Nick with pleading, tear-filled eyes, which alternated with her gaze of tempered steel. Her eyes traced down to the cornmeal on the floor. Nick looked back at the tapestry. He knew he had to leave. They both had to leave. He reached down and picked her up in his arms like a baby. Whatever bullshit was happening on the floor needed to forgotten. They needed to get away. Nick walked to the door with Euri in his arms and kicked it open. He took one more glance at the transom, and then walked out the door over the line of cornmeal, placing his non-skid, non-marking, oil-resistant sole directly upon it.

Outside, the wind was blowing furiously. A coyote howled in the distance.

16

The Departure

They walked toward the short pass at the south end of the mountain. It would take them out of the meadow and down from the mountain, back toward Seligman. Angry clouds swirled above them. In the time it took to leave the shack and reach the exit from the valley, the clouds had entirely covered the peaks that held the shrine.

Snow had started to accumulate near the trees. Nick held Euri close under his arm as they walked. The wind buffeted them. They were silent. Occasionally, the urge to effuse about something positive in Chicago came to him, but those urges were instantly, ferociously beaten down inside of him before he made a sound.

They had both lost a father. Bacho had provided Nick with the reassurance that he had lacked as a child. Bacho had driven him to confront his own fears, and had seen into his soul. Bacho had saved his life. Nick had repaid him by taking his. But the sense that it had all been foretold in the tapestries overwhelmed Nick. As he looked at Euri, he felt she held a wisdom beyond any event of the last few minutes.

They walked up the short rise and into the wooded area between two lower peaks. Nick kept his eyes on the trail. The path got rougher. Nick tried to imagine what it must have been like for Bacho, poor Bacho, to have dragged him all that distance over that terrain. It had been not only the weight of Nick's comatose body but also a guitar and a few books for Euri that Bacho was dragging behind him on the travois. Descending was difficult enough for the two of them, both relatively young and unencumbered. The ascent was almost unthinkable.

Bacho, the old Indian guy who had seen with more than his eyes. Nick's mind still spun, still trying to grasp the tapestries. He surrendered to the idea of them. Ever since he'd left Amarillo on this trip, nothing had made any sense. His rational nature had been more or less destroyed when he awoke in a shack to find himself attended by an old Indian guy and his beautiful daughter. Even now, feeling still battled reason inside of him. Was this really happening? He had decided to surrender to it, to ride it out. It had been a conscious decision. He was trying to see in other ways.

He looked down at Euri at his side. Her eyes rose to his. They were still tear-stained, but the adversity she and Nick faced on the trail had turned her expression into one of stoic determination.

They stepped over trees across the path. They had recently fallen in the storm. The wind whipped up dust and debris with the snowflakes. They shook their heads and wiped their eyes. They kept walking. Euri grasped Nick's hand tightly.

Above them and to the right of the trail was the mountain with the shrine to Hehewuti and the other ancestors. Nick gazed up at it as they walked past. Euri didn't. Nick wondered how it must feel for her to be leaving her home in the shadow of her mother's memorial. It was impossible to tell by looking at her. He couldn't see in the way he was used to seeing. It was impossible to apply reason and logic to this situation. He tried to feel, instead. In silence, they walked on.

Finally, Euri spoke. "This is the day the Hopi say that spirits come down from the mountain. They take people over, on this day. My dad never followed Hopi ways, really, but he said it was important for my mother's people. So, he always remembered."

Nick didn't know what to say. He looked at her and frowned.

"Do you believe he's with his ancestors now? Your ancestors, I mean?" he asked.

"I think," she said, plainly, softly, but then seemed to reconsider her choice of words. "I believe he *is* the mountain now." They walked on in silence for a ways. "Maybe it's the same thing, really."

"Yes," said Nick. "Because we are all made of stars. Everything is made of stars. Stardust."

It was still a beautiful image to Nick, regardless of what had just happened in the shack. He remembered the night that Bacho had first told him about stardust. Then he remembered the many other times when he accompanied Bacho as he gathered sheep or stones or firewood, hearing tales of those who came before. He remembered the one time he joined Bacho on a deer hunt in a small gorge. It reminded him of his time in Belgium so much that he almost felt the dead spot rising up within him again. Nick had gazed up as the sun was setting and the vast fields of stars were just starting to peek through the deepening blue mantle of the sky. In those times he saw how both he and Bacho were only two stars that "moved different," and that somehow they had always been and always would be. They were stardust—eternal in their own ways.

Euri pursed her lips, then smiled, and nodded.

They walked on.

As they clambered over another limestone ridge, Nick thought he heard Euri crying. She was in front of him. Softly, he called her name. She turned. Her expression was sad but calm. "Are you OK?" he asked. She looked questioningly, then smiled and nodded.

Her eyes were as beautiful as ever. They were emerging from sadness. There was a certain fullness to her face he hadn't noticed before. She was still utterly beautiful—enough to stop his heart. Perhaps it was the trauma of the last hour that had caused him to see her as even more of a woman. He had known she had the daring and resolve to leave, but he honestly hadn't thought that her strength would still sustain her. She had just seen the death of her own father at the hands of her husband. Nick was further convinced of a deep wisdom in her. She had seen life in other ways.

They walked on. Nick could see the wind whipping snow around the side of a cliff to their right. The sky was a tumultuous patchwork of morning sunshine and dark, swirling clouds. They walked along the base of the cliff. Nick got a sense that they were nearing a summit that would reveal more beyond.

"Euri, what was the grain for?" Nick asked.

"Grain?"

"Yes, the powder your father spilled in the doorway. At the shack. Cornmeal?"

Euri gathered her thoughts. She spoke deliberately. "The Hopi believe in a white brother they call Pahana. He went east sometime long ago. They are still waiting for him to return. He's supposed to come back wearing red and unite everyone—all religions. All tribes. He's supposed to bring East and West together. My father thought you might be him."

"I know," he told me. But I think he decided I wasn't."

"Yes, I think he decided no," she reflected. After a few more steps, she said, "But then the cornmeal was sacred. Pahana can walk over it. If you weren't Pahana, you weren't supposed to be able to cross it. It would have stopped you from leaving. So, he was testing."

"That's an old legend," said Nick, recalling how he deliberately stepped on the yellow grain on the transom. "I mean, you don't believe that, right?"

Euri kept walking. She tilted her head. "I don't follow all my mother's ways—the ways of the Hopi," she said, finally. "Neither did my mother, really. But it was important to her. It was important to honor her mothers."

They walked on. Nick started to feel more conversational. He felt his strength coming back to him, his presence and awareness increasing. He was getting more curious. He felt himself emerging from a shell.

"When you two were shouting, you said something to him in a very angry voice. That was just before he grabbed you." Nick didn't know if he was within his rights. "What was that about?"

"It was about the bad time. The bad time with the missionaries, I mean...the..."

Nick waited for her to explain. They walked on in silence. Maybe she wasn't ready. Nick would let it slide. For now.

They had just cleared the side of the cliff and suddenly the valley lay out before them. Clouds still washed through the sky, and the light snow fell, still driven by cold winds. Nick was almost elated. He could see through the clouds and into the valley. He thought he could see the outlines of some structures below. He paused to look hard through the wind-driven mist. He pointed off in the distance.

"Euri! We're getting close! I think I see the highway! Maybe over there, where it's dark, you see?" He pointed at a far-off line, almost invisible behind the mist. He turned to look at her. She looked at him with joy. He looked in her eyes and noticed something for the first time: The smile lines on the side of her face. Back when he opened his eyes and saw her on that first day, when he regained his sight, he saw a round-eyed child. Now, she was very obviously a woman. His heart swelled. She had grown just in the time they had been together. She was a woman now. He began to think of her carrying his child. He kissed her.

As he kissed her, he heard a distant howl that sounded almost like a deep cry. He pulled back and looked around. Only sparse juniper trees surrounded them. It seemed the sound was coming from behind them. Nick told himself it was only the wind rushing through the trees or some narrow gorge in the mountains behind them—the mountain of the shrine. He turned toward the path. They walked on.

The trail was very rough as it descended onto the mesa. They were traversing narrow paths and even clambering over boulders. Nick offered Euri his hand as she walked over them. Finally, they were on something resembling level ground.

"We've made it this far. Let's take a break," said Nick.

It was cold and the wind still blew. They took shelter under a juniper tree. Nick opened the leather knapsack and pulled out a cloth holding some cornbread and cooked lamb. He gave it to Euri. He unplugged one of the botas and offered it to her. She declined but took a bite of cornbread. Nick took a drink.

He watched her eat. He missed those whorls on the side of her head. He knew it was customary only for unmarried girls to wear their hair that way, but there was such a cuteness to them. From the moment he first saw them, to the day they had first taken each other, or, rather, she had taken him, they had been like a third member of their relationship. He ran his fingers through her ponytail. He had never noticed gray hairs before. The whorls had probably concealed them. Not that he didn't like the gray, and he wouldn't recommend that she wear the whorls again just for vanity's sake. He started to wonder what she would wear in Chicago. Would she dress in the mode of the day? A little A-line dress like Harriet Nelson, her hair in some close cut perm? Would they have a house in Lake Forest or Evanston? Would she be a joiner and fit in with the ladies who lunch, bringing her own exotic flavor to the dull drabness of white suburban life? What would they say back there?

Or, maybe that wouldn't work. Maybe they would need to live in an apartment around a university or a college where their odd combination would be welcomed by other disparate couples in some bohemian enclave. Nick's mind raced. Maybe he could go back to college, getting a degree in literature or political science. Maybe even American Indian studies. What a handle he would have on that! He could write a book already. Maybe he could get a graduate degree and take up teaching. And Euri, after some remedial instruction, could join him in his quest for knowledge. She was so bright that she could be the toast of the town. That could work out. It really could!

Nick's mind started to race with plans for the future. He couldn't remember when he had last felt this way. It was as if he was standing at the top of a cyclone, looking into this swirling funnel of infinite possibilities. He heard the sound again, distant, powerful, seemingly angry and sad and joyous all at once. Tones mixed. It was a deep bass combined with a high, lilting almost-whistle.

Wind, he thought.

Nick watched Euri as she ate. She paused now and then to pick out the little bits of juniper that had fallen in the cornbread. He looked at her and didn't see a little girl anymore. He saw a mature

woman—the mother of his beautiful little Greek/
Irish/Indian children—harried but not unhappy
as she chased them around a little two-bedroom
apartment and Nick typed out the latest copy of
his manuscript, a pipe stuffed with tobacco sitting
on the desk in a little purpose-built pipe holder.
He'd lean back thoughtfully and maybe catch one
of the kids as he or she ran by, admonishing them
to mind their mother. Euri looked back at him
and smiled and reached and for the water in his
hands. He looked at her hands. They weren't the
childish little mitts he had seen wiping his face
only a few weeks before. These were the hands of
a woman. He imagined them arranging the hair of
a beautiful little girl into the whorls he had found
so charming. The Family Pente would keep the
traditions, at least enough to pass them on to the
next generation.

Nick looked up at the storm, still blowing snow
through the juniper. He got to his feet, brushed off
his pants, and offered his hand to Euri. She didn't
immediately spring to her feet. He lent her a hand.
They had already been walking for a few hours.
Even Nick himself felt strained.

"Let's keep going. We're going to Chicago." Nick
smiled. "Sweet home, Chicago!" He laughed. Euri
laughed. "You know that song? Did I ever sing you
that song?" She shook her head and smiled.

"Nick, sing your song. The wheel song."

"Perry Como?"

"Yes, Perry."

Nick started walking, and if he ever thought he could actually sing a song, it was that song, at just that time. He sang his heart out.

Find a wheel and it goes round, round, round,
As it skims along with a happy sound!
As it goes along the ground, ground, ground,
Till it leads you to the one you love!

Euri smiled and held Nick's hand. They were almost skipping together through the storm. Euri started singing with him, her lightly accented English adding a delightful flavor to the song that was so caucasian white that it almost burned like a magnesium fire.

Still, they sang. They were now off the mountain, and the walking was easier, but the storm still blew. Visions ran through Nick's head: filmclips of joyous Christmas mornings and romantic afternoons spent near the lakeshore. Visions of university junkets spent touring old Indian ruins. He imagined Polaroids and station wagons. There would be nights when he'd curl up with her in bed after writing or lecturing or researching so much that he could barely move, much less think. His life would now start. The first thirty-two years had only been a prelude.

"Nick, I want to ask you a question."

"Sure, honey."

"Well, first I want to say I am sorry for calling you a coward."

Nick paused to think back. After several more steps, he finally recalled what she meant. "You mean a *charibovi?*" Nick laughed. Euri joined him, embarrassed. "Forget it," he said. "Water under the bridge."

"Well, good. I want to say that I am sorry for saying that about your father."

Nick didn't at first recall what she was referring to in this case, either. Then, he remembered that confrontation near the well. What if he had known that his leaving home would mean he'd lose both his mother and his father—the man who had more or less raised him? What if he knew his leaving would cause it all?

"Euri, I know what you meant. I know." Nick thought it over more. He remembered that until only a few hours earlier, he had an adoptive father of sorts. And one decisive moment had seemingly changed it all. He thought back on the moment he found out his mother had died and his shock at finding his father dead the day after. He wondered how many of his own decisions were part of the path that led to those events. Or if his decisions had even really mattered at all.

"Euri, there's not much I regret," said Nick, lying to her and himself. "My dad made his decision. I'm just glad he was around when I needed him to be around. Just like Bacho was for you."

"Then, Nick," she continued. "What do you regret?"

Euri stopped. Nick turned to look at her. The lines around her face were showing more deeply now. The stress and the weather were making her look much older than her nineteen or twenty years. He picked some snowflakes off her hair. The snowflakes were making her look gray. She looked into his eyes.

Nick thought back to when he was sixteen. And again, when he was eighteen. And again, a year or so later—to that day in Belgium.

"Euri, when I was young, I had this problem," he began. "I had it for a long time. I still do from time to time." Euri looked concerned. Nick took a deep breath. "You see, I have these times when my world, when everything just kinda stops for me. It's like it's in suspended animation. It used to happen only when I was scared. Then, for a long time, it seemed to happen just whenever. But, mainly, when I was scared about something or something was making me..." Nick tried to paraphrase something Dr. Kultra had told him. "When I coped with my anxiety, my fear, by forgetting that I existed. My mind would pretend that I didn't exist anymore, and I had become like a...thing. So, when these times happen, it can be dangerous. Because I don't know what's going on around me, in a lot of ways. I just freeze."

Euri nodded as she looked at her moccasins making footprints in the light dusting of snow on the path.

"So, when I went to sneak into the army, my dad knew I had this problem. And that's a big part of the reason he didn't want me to go. He knew what it was. He wanted me to stay for his own reasons, but he also didn't think that I could make it in the army. He knew I had this problem. And he probably didn't think I would last."

"So, why are you sorry about that?" asked Euri. The snow was really starting to accumulate on her hair. Nick felt his brow furrow.

"Euri, it's this..." He breathed heavily. "I went to the army when I was eighteen, before they drafted me. They asked some very specific questions about my health and about what sorts of treatments I had. And so, I really wanted to get into the army and get away from my mom and dad. So, I lied. I told them I was fine. No problems. My Sergeant knew I had problems. So one day in Belgium, the day with the German, I froze up. I dropped my gun. I didn't know what I was doing. He pulled me behind some cover. Then, when he was trying to help me, he got shot. He got killed right in front of me." Nick exhaled. "And it was all my fault."

Euri paused, looked at up Nick, then walked on alone in front of him. Nick noticed her gait had changed. There was a little sway in it. The winds were blowing so hard by then. The trail was getting harder to see. Nick wanted to give her some distance to think over what he had revealed. After a few minutes, Euri's pace slowed. Nick caught up beside her. She looked at him.

"Nick, that was your friend's decision. Not yours." She was almost shouting over the wind.

"It was my decision. I had the flaw. I didn't tell anyone."

"You didn't force him to do anything. He decided to help you. It was his job. He was a soldier."

"He thought I was OK. I had passed the physical."

"And what did you do after your sergeant was killed? You saved your friends. You saved them. Right?"

She stopped.

Nick looked at Euri. He took her hand. It was strangely thin, and some marks—spots—had appeared on the back. He looked into her eyes. She had taken on some deep aura of wisdom that he couldn't place. It was different than what he had known from her before. She was present with him in some new way. He was suddenly aware. He could see himself through her eyes: the man she loved. The man worth loving. The man worth losing everything she had called "home" before. He stammered and moved around on his feet back and forth. He felt something welling up in his throat.

He turned and started walking, deep in thought. She followed.

She started to sing in her little native-inflected voice, slightly off-key at first. Her voice seemed to be taking on an odd, gravelly tone:

Find a wheel and it goes round, round, round
As it skims along with a happy sound.

Tears welled up in Nick's eyes. They could have been melting snowflakes, he told himself. He walked on, looking far off in the distance toward the road. He started to sing with Euri, keeping his voice soft so he could hear hers.

Nick heard the far-off sound again, crying in the distance. It seemed to be harmonizing with them in some way. Or, at least Nick thought so.

"The wind! It's singing with us!" Nick laughed. Euri looked up at him and smiled sweetly.

They approached a rocky section of the trail and moved to single file. Nick kept walking until he realized that Euri wasn't close behind him. She was getting tired. The terrain had gotten rougher. He hiked back to her. Now, he noticed there was a stoop to her back. She had to deliberately look up at him. He put his hands around her waist and smiled at her. There were lines and spots on her face. But as he looked her in the eyes, he only saw one thing. He only saw someone who had stripped away every sin, every flaw, every misstep and mistake and missed opportunity and every other reason he had found to hate and doubt himself. It seemed that every bad thing in him had been replaced with hope and joy.

He felt her hips through the skirt. He felt more bone than flesh. He didn't think about it. He was more full of life than he ever had been before.

He held her hand as they kept walking. They were back on level ground and walked more and more slowly, side by side, now with his hand around her waist, and holding her hand in his. He looked down at the top of her head. It was getting whiter and whiter. Still they walked on. And Nick softly sang with Euri:

Then your love will hold you round, round, round
In your heart's a song with a brand new sound
And your head goes spinning round, round, round
'cause you've found what you've been dreamin' of.

And the wind still howled.

They got to a rise in a clearing between the junipers. As they slowly crested it, Nick stopped. He heard something.

"Euri, you hear that?" It was hard to hear anything over the wind in the trees and the far-off howling in the background.

Euri looked up at him, her eyes dimmed by cataracts, lines covering her face. "What?" she asked.

"Euri! That sound!" Nick recognized the sound made by the diesel trucks as they decelerated. It was a specific sort of *ratttttattttattt*. He had heard it for years. Engine braking.

"It's a truck! Euri! We're almost there! We're almost at Seligman! We made it!" He grasped both of her hands. Slowly a smile came over her face, little darts of joy in her eyes. Nick looked at her and saw only the girl who woke him with her damp cloth on his forehead.

"Let's go! Let's go now! We'll flag down a ride. Let's run! Euri!" Nick was almost jumping.

"Nick, I . . . I can't." Her voice had taken on a shudder.

"That's OK. I'll carry you." Nick reached down before she could protest and picked her up. Through the thick wool fabric of her skirt and poncho, he thought he could feel the bones of her hips and ribs against his arms. She looked in his eyes lovingly and smiled. He sang again.

Find a ring and put it round, round, round,
And with ties so strong that two hearts are bound!
Put it on the one you've found, found, found!
For you know that his is really love!

Nick walked as fast and evenly as he could, taking care to keep his footsteps sure and smooth. He heard another truck and the whooshing sound of a passing car. The howl from the wind was getting louder as well. He dropped the bags so he could hold Euri more firmly. He cleared another patch of juniper, and then the road was before him, no more than one hundred feet away. He felt his heart beating with hers. He scanned to his left and right. They were sure to get a ride easily. Off to his left, he could see the Texaco station in the distance, where the men had confronted him back then. That seemed like ages ago. It was close enough to reach on foot. He was now almost running toward the road, Euri in his arms. He looked straight ahead. Euri's hand, now old and withered, reached up to his chest. He looked down. They were almost to the roadside now, with Nick just scrambling over the last of some brambles. The wind was blowing furiously. The howling sound had gotten even louder, the *basso-profondo* rumbling competing with the high screeching. The clouds fought the sun above them, waging war in the atmosphere.

He looked at Euri, lying in his arms. She was now an ancient woman, with eyes almost completely covered in cataracts, her lips dried and wrinkled, her cheekbones showing through skin darkened by liver spots. He saw only beauty. He saw only Euri as she was when he first saw her in the cabin. She gestured for him. He moved his head near her.

"Nick," her voice was very soft, very frail. He could barely hear her over the sound of the howling in the background. It was a distorted baritone wailing at this point. "Nick."

"Yes, Euri, yes?"

"You must know, you are..."

"Yes? Do you need water?"

"You must know...you must know this..." Her voice started to trail off. He looked at her intently, his lips shuddering. She stared at him in adoration. "Nick, you are loved. I love you. Now, you must love all...and most of all...love yourself. But first, you must forgive all. And know...that you are forgiven."

Her eyes, still shining forth in their brown-saffron beauty through the cataracts, closed one last time, just as she smiled. Nick looked at her and leaned to kiss her. "Euri, I love you," he said, softly, his heart palpitating and his lips trembling. Her smiled brightened, then she moved no more.

Nick gazed at her. He felt some force swirling within him, up from his center, propagating through his spine. It came from the center and coursed through every vein, every capillary, every nerve and sinew in his body. It had started as a warm glow at the bottom of his abdomen, and now he felt it in each extremity. It encapsulated every moment of rage, of fear, of abandonment, and of joy he could ever remember feeling. It contained every last urge of hate and love and desire he had ever felt. It started in his center, and glowed as it increased in a swirl, propagating as it moved outward.

He looked up at the swirling, angry clouds in the sky and the great blue beyond that they fought to conceal.

He took a deep breath. And then something moved within him, driving the air out from his lungs and through his vocal chords, all of his parts conspiring to create a tone of absolute certainty. "I am Nicholas Constantin Pentangeloi, I am of Greek descent, a veteran of the Battle of the Bulge, decorated war hero, son of an optician and a beautiful, drunken Irishwoman. I am a musician, long-distance driver, and beloved husband of Euri, whom I love more than life itself. I am aware." Nick gulped. "And I love..." He gasped as the tears began to flow. *"And I...love...and...and I forgive myself and...all others."*

He realized he was standing beside a sign. He gazed upwards. It said, "Arizona U.S. 66." His mind raced back to the image that had been at the center of the steering wheel of his truck: The red *T*.

The howling had reached a tremendous, thrashing crescendo. He knew it was approaching from behind him. He slowly turned back to look at the mountain he and Euri had descended together only hours before. He saw it rimmed by an aura of light, fluctuating through all colors and intensities. The whole mountain seemed to be resonating from within, the sound now almost deafening. He felt something change – the sensation in his arms. He looked down to see Euri's body had crumbled to dust in his hands, leaving him holding only her skirt and blouse, which then faded and fragmented to threads.

Then, his own hands slowly became grains of white dust as well, starting from his fingertips, with the grains gently falling together beneath him with the dust that was Euri.

And as he watched himself become dust, all gently faded to white.

The atmosphere went still. A car drove by. The sound of the howling was replaced by the buzz of tires on asphalt, rapidly retreating to the west from beneath the wheels of the rusty, grey Studebaker. In a moment the clouds retreated, and finally there was the low sun illuminating the remains of a perfect, blue afternoon sky.

But just as the air displaced by that rusty gray 1948 Studebaker Champion coupe with luggage strapped to the roof reached the mound of dust beside the road, and just as it had begun to disperse the first few grains off the top, a blast of wind came down from the mountain. It was nearly as focused as a beam of light, and seemed to travel almost as fast. When it reached the side of the road, it stopped short, spiraling into a miniature vortex directly over where Nick and Euri had stood. The small whirlwind spun beside the road, growing as it lifted their dust and mixed it with the sand from the ground and little bits of juniper and scrub oak and dry grass. It quickly gained size and momentum as it howled in the combined tones of high and low frequencies.

Then, the growing, howling cyclone lifted up off the ground—slowly rising higher and higher in the air.

The sudden winds buffeted the Studebaker. It made it weave in its lane. In the car, a young man with long, greasy hair and sunglasses glanced up, then stared into the rear-view mirror. He saw the dustdevil spinning—now a large cyclone. He gaped as he took his cigarette out of his mouth.

"Hey, Sher: Look at that—behind us. It's like--*a tornado.*"

His groggy companion lifted herself from her repose against the window, a paperback Jorge Luis Borges anthology on her chest. She was carefully holding her cigarette as she twisted in her seat to look out the back window. "Oh Troy! Oh wow, that could have *killed* us!"

Troy turned back to the road just in time to see the torpedo-like nose of the Studebaker aiming straight for the left front fender of a dirty brown 1955 Peterbilt semi-tractor travelling in the opposite direction. Both car and truck were overlapping the centerline of the highway.

Sher screamed as Troy yanked the wheel to the right and the car lunged. The car flipped onto its roof as the front tire tucked under. Sparks flew and metal shredded as it slid into a ditch, a trail of gasoline spilling behind it. The suitcases ripped from the roof rack, scattering their contents as they split open. The Peterbilt veered, briefly tipping up on its right-side wheels, then slammed over as the trailer yanked the tractor to the ground, sliding down the highway and spilling its cargo of decaffeinated coffee across Route 66 as the steel panels ripped and burst.

The truck slid to a halt, wheels still spinning. After a few moments, the driver's side door of the truck slowly flipped up. The driver, still dazed from the crash, emerged through the haze of steam and smoke, shaking. He beheld the devastation through dilated pupils and a disbelieving sneer.

"Holy shit," he gasped in a tremulous voice, a shaking hand rising to slick back his dark, greased hair. He gazed at the smoking wreck of the Studebaker in the ditch. "Shit..." He heard moans and cries. The fire had started. "Shit..." Shaking, he took a seat on the flat surface of the sleeper cab and lit a cigarette, taking time to assess the situation, and whether he should get involved, and the possible consequences for him if he did, and whether he had any choice at this point. His head turned. He looked behind him and up at the cyclone that had distracted him for one fatal moment. It continued to rise through the air, still spinning, gaining size and power. "*Shit. ..*"

With the screech of tires on pavement, a white Buick slid to a stop beside the truck. A man flung the door open, jumped out, and ran towards the burning Studebaker, ripping off his blue windbreaker and wrapping it around his forearm as he ran.

The truck driver looked at the man. There was something unexpected about him—something unusual and even threatening. The truck driver got to his feet. He was emboldened with nervous energy. Rage overwhelmed him. He stood on the side of the truck and angrily pointed and shouted at the man.

"Boy! Boy! Just who the hell do you think you are, boy? Are you *aware . . ."*

17

Newsflash

AP WIRE SERVICE

DATELINE: DECEMBER 22, 1957
SELIGMAN, ARIZONA.

A BIZARRE EARTHQUAKE-LIKE EVENT
SHOOK RESIDENTS OF THIS TINY DES-
ERT COMMUNITY YESTERDAY, AND THREE
WERE HURT IN A COLLISION BETWEEN A
PASSENGER CAR AND A TRACTOR-TRAIL-
ER ON ROUTE 66, EAST OF TOWN, IN WHAT
MIGHT HAVE BEEN A RELATED EVENT.
    AREA RESIDENTS OVERLOADED POLICE
AND FIRE SWITCHBOARDS WITH REPORTS

OF TREMORS, LOUD HUMMING SOUNDS AND FLASHES OF LIGHT FROM MOUNTAINS IN THE AREA. THE ACTIVITY WAS FIRST REPORTED AT AROUND 4:00 P.M. LOCAL TIME.

"I COULD HEAR THIS BUZZING SOUND, AND THEN THE LIGHTS WENT OUT FOR A WHILE. THE DOGS WAS [SIC] BARKING" SAID SELIGMAN RESIDENT JOHN HAYES, 67. "I THOUGHT IT WAS THE END OF THE WORLD, OR MAYBE ANOTHER TRAIN CRASH."

SEISMOGRAPHS AT NEARBY NORTHERN ARIZONA UNIVERSITY RECORDED A SMALL TREMOR OF ABOUT 2.1 ON THE RICHTER SCALE AT AROUND 4:00 P.M. GEOLOGY PROFESSOR DR. IRWIN CANDLE, PHD STATED THAT SUCH TREMORS ARE NOT UNUSUAL. HE OFFERED NO EXPLANATION FOR MYSTERIOUS LIGHTS OR SOUNDS.

SANTA FE RAILOAD REPORTED NORMAL OPERATIONS ALONG THE CHICAGO-LOS ANGELES ROUTE. NEITHER THE AIR FORCE NOR CIVIL AVIATION AUTHORITIES REPORTED ANY MISSING AIRCRAFT IN THE AREA. THE AEC AT THE NEVADA PROVING GROUNDS HAD NO REPORTS OF ANY ATOMIC WEAPONS TESTS IN PROGRESS AS OF YESTERDAY AFTERNOON.

A CRASH BETWEEN A WESTBOUND PAS-SENGER CAR AND AN EASTBOUND TRAC-TOR-TRAILER WAS REPORTED AROUND 4:15

PM. INJURED WERE STUDENTS TROY VANA-
RSDALE, 22, OF LOS ANGELES, CALIFORNIA,
AND SHARILYN HIMMELFARB, 23, OF LIN-
COLNWOOD, ILLINOIS. AUTHORITIES
PRAISED THE ACTIONS OF UNEMPLOYED
DOCKWORKER SHELBY HOWELL, 26, OF
LONG BEACH, CALIFORNIA. HE PULLED
BOTH STUDENTS FROM THE WRECK OF
THEIR 1948 STUDEBAKER COUPE BEFORE
THE GAS TANK EXPLODED. BOTH ARE CUR-
RENTLY RECOVERING AT MOJAVE COUNTY
HOSPITAL IN KINGMAN.   MR. HOWELL
RECEIVED ONLY MINOR BURNS.

IN A GESTURE OF HOLIDAY GOODWILL,
LOCAL BUSINESSES AWARDED MR. HOWELL
WITH GAS AND TIRES TO ASSIST WITH
HIS TRIP HOME TO HIS FAMILY IN LONG
BEACH.

SOON AFTER HIGHWAY PATROL AND
FIRE CREWS ARRIVED AT THE SCENE,
TRUCK DRIVER JED STEWART, 38, OF
TALLAHASSEE, FLORIDA, WAS DETAINED
FOR WHAT WAS DESCRIBED AS "ODD
BEHAVIOR". IT WAS LATER DISCOVERED
THAT MR. STEWART HAD WARRANTS IN
SEVERAL STATES FOR INDECENT ASSAULT,
STATUTORY   RAPE   AND   NARCOTICS.
SEVERAL   SUITCASES   FOUND   NEAR
THE SCENE WERE FOUND FILLED WITH
HASHISH, MARIJUANA, BENZEDRINE, AND
OTHER ILLEGAL NARCOTICS.

ROUTE 66 WAS EXPECTED TO BE OPEN AGAIN FOR TWO-WAY TRAFFIC BY THE TIME OF PUBLICATION.

THE COLLISION REMINDED LOCAL RESIDENTS OF THE CRASH IN THE EARLY HOURS OF NOVEMBER 14TH BETWEEN A TRACTOR-TRAILER AND THE EASTBOUND SANTA FE SUPER CHIEF, CLAIMING THE DRIVER'S LIFE, DERAILING THE TRAIN, AND CREATING LONG DELAYS FOR TRAVELLERS.

DRIVER NICHOLAS C. PENTE, 32, OF CHICAGO, ILLINOIS, WAS BEHIND THE WHEEL OF THE TRACTOR-TRAILER WHEN IT LEFT U.S. 66 WHILE CROSSING AN OVERPASS AT APPROXIMATELY 5:15 A.M. ENGINEERS OF THE SUPER CHIEF, WHICH WAS CARRYING 603 PASSENGERS AT THE TIME, DIDN'T GET SUFFICIENT WARNING TO AVOID COLLIDING WITH THE TRUCK, WHICH WAS HANGING FROM THE BRIDGE'S SPAN. INJURIES AMONG THE CREW AND PASSENGERS OF THE SUPER CHIEF WERE MINOR. BUSES WERE SENT FROM KINGMAN AND FLAGSTAFF TO FERRY THE PASSENGERS TO THE NEXT STOP ON THE SUPER CHIEF'S ROUTE TO CHICAGO. IT HAD DEPARTED ITS PREVIOUS STOP IN KINGMAN ONLY AN HOUR BEFORE THE COLLISION.

INITIAL REPORTS STATED THAT THE TRUCK CARRIED HAZARDOUS CARGO, AND

LOCAL AUTHORITIES WERE WARNED TO EVACUATE THE AREA BY TWO VISITING MEMBERS OF THE ATOMIC ENERGY COMMISSION WHO HAPPENED TO BE IN THE AREA ON ANOTHER INVESTIGATION. IT WAS LATER LEARNED THAT THE TRAILER HAD CARRIED ONLY PAPER PRODUCTS.

"THOUGH THERE IS NO HAZARDOUS CARGO, WE ADVISE ONGOING CAUTION IN THE AREA OF THE TRAILER COLLISION," STATED AEC SPOKESMAN DR. HENRIK MÜHLBAUER. "THAT IS THE MESSAGE. LOCAL CITIZENS HAVE THE KEY TO THEIR OWN SAFETY AND WELL-BEING."

MÜHLBAUER WAS UNAVAILABLE TO COMMENT ON THE SEISMIC EVENTS OF YESTERDAY AFTERNOON.

AS OF THIS WRITING, LOCAL AUTHORI-TIES STILL WISH TO SPEAK TO AN OLDER INDIAN MAN WHO WAS WITNESSED NEAR THE LOCATION OF THE CRASH BY SANTA FE ENGINEERS IMMEDIATELY AFTER IMPACT.

THE DRIVER'S BODY WAS NOT FOUND WITHIN THE WRECKAGE OF THE TRUCK. IT IS ASSUMED THAT IT WAS INCINERATED IN THE EXPLOSION.

CONCERNED RESIDENTS ALSO REPORT-ED TWO BRIGHT OBJECTS IN THE EARLY EVENING SKY THAT APPEARED TO CON-VERGE INTO A SINGLE POINT OF LIGHT,

HIGH IN THE ATMOSPHERE. SOME RESI-
DENTS REPORTED SEEING THE LIGHT JET-
TING SKYWARD LIKE A ROCKET BEFORE
DISAPPEARING INTO SPACE. AUTHORI-
TIES STATE THAT THESE WERE LIKELY
ORDINARY METEORITES AND WERE NOT
RELATED TO THE OTHER EVENTS.

THE END

Afterword and Acknowledgements

This book sprang from me fully formed—like Athena from the head of Zeus—one hot afternoon when I was walking around downtown Valencia, Spain, in 1992.

Part of that explanation is factual, and even the part that isn't fact is still true in a mythical way.

The core idea of blending mythologies—European and Amerindian, ancient and modern—came to me when I saw an "Arizona Route 66" license plate on a motor scooter in Spain that spring day. It just took 20 years or so for the rest to come together. Maybe that's the difference between time on earth among mortals versus time on Olympus among the gods. Or perhaps even time in the mythical mountains above Seligman, Arizona versus time on a calendar.

There is almost nothing factual in this book, but of the few facts or fact-like appurtenances here, there are some real doozies.

Yes, the U.S. government had a top-secret mind-control program in the 1950s. It sought out people with nervous disorders as well as victims of childhood sexual abuse, plied them with drugs, put them under hypnosis, then put them to work, observing them to try and discover some ultimate means of control that might be used on enemies, or that enemies might use on Americans. The name of the program was MKULTRA. I think you can see how that turns up in this text. And yes, the U.S. secretly imported and patriated former Nazis to work in not only the space program, but the post-war intelligence and medical research communities as well.

There was never any "Heartland" in Flagstaff. I don't know if there was an "EAT" in Acoma. I'm almost sure there was never a "Jet" outside of Amarillo, nor a "Navajo Acres" outside of Ash Fork. Those places are amalgams of the roadside culture of the times, and in their own ways reflect the myths of modern America along the mythic Route 66. If you go looking for remnants of these places (and I suggest you do) don't expect to find them as described. But go anyway: You might find something even cooler.

As far as the Indian ethnography goes, some of it gibes. Hopi families are matrilineal, with possessions passed down from the mother's side. There is an old Hopi belief in a Pahana figure--a lost white brother that returns from the East. The Spaniards and various missionaries tried to exploit that belief to dominate the Hopi. It is said that spirits come down from the mountain during the winter solstice. The Hopi men weave rugs, though the fineness of the tapestries described here is otherworldly.

I'd like to thank my mother, who whacked me on the head with a broom until I started writing on my own when she was teaching me 4th grade. I thank my father as well, mainly for exploding in anger when I told him I wanted to be a lawyer.

I'd like to recognize a few other people for their assistance and inspiration: Sean Ellis, Jeremy and Kara Beer, the sisters Coe (both Kathryn and Anne), Dan and Diane Sorensen, Alexis Astorga, and of course, Edward Georgevich, without whose help this book would have been far different.

Most of all, I thank Blair Coe Schweiger, who wouldn't let me forget that I had always wanted to get this story down on paper and provided many insights on Indian ways. It's a great help to have a writing friend who's an anthropologist (among other things).

--Phoenix, May 2014

www.ingramcontent.com/pod-product-compliance
Lightning Source LLC
Chambersburg PA
CBHW022113240626
47153CB00007B/2346